THE ITALIAN LAKE

Anna Villiers is granddaughter of the founder of Villiers Properties and Estates. When she is forced to merge with rival Phil Anderson sparks fly between them from the very first day. Phil suspects Anna of colluding against him with local property developer Archie Wainwright, but Anna has a family secret which she cannot reveal — even at the risk of losing her job, as well as her heart to Phil Anderson . . .

Books by Margaret Mounsdon
in the Linford Romance Library:

THE MIMOSA SUMMER

WL

Please return/renew this item by the last date shown

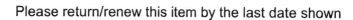
worcestershire
countycouncil
Libraries & Learning

MARGARET MOUNSDON

THE ITALIAN LAKE

Complete and Unabridged

LINFORD
Leicester

First published in Great Britain in 2009

First Linford Edition
published 2010

British Library CIP Data

Mounsdon, Margaret.
 The Italian lake. - -
 (Linford romance library)
 1. Real estate agents- -Fiction.
 2. Love stories.
 3. Large type books.
 I. Title II. Series
 823.9′2–dc22

 ISBN 978–1–84782–986–3

Published by
F. A. Thorpe (Publishing)
Anstey, Leicestershire

Set by Words & Graphics Ltd.
Anstey, Leicestershire
Printed and bound in Great Britain by
T. J. International Ltd., Padstow, Cornwall

This book is printed on acid-free paper

A Shock For Anna

Anna grimaced as mud squelched over her high-heeled shoes. She put out a hand and grabbed a moss-covered gatepost. The wind was doing a marvellous job of ruining her hair-do, and she watched in dismay as the estate agent's particulars were whipped out of her hand by a goat.

'Here, give that back,' she protested, as the animal skipped away leaving a trail of shredded paper behind it. It floated away in the breeze like confetti at a wedding.

Fuming, Anna looked round at the sodden landscape. The view was panoramic but today she had no eyes for the rolling hills and green fields. All she could think about was that years of poor harvests and economic legislation had forced the owners of Hillcrest Farm into selling up. Anna knew how desperate they must be. Her own family history mirrored that of Hillcrest Farm and if it hadn't been for Phil Anderson coming to her father's rescue, they would have been forced to sell up their family business, too.

But dwelling on the past wasn't going to get her out of her present trouble. Her mouth tightened as she thought of Phil Anderson. Tall, good-looking, ambitious and charming, a charm that he used by the bucket-load when it suited him.

Anna remembered their first encounter, when he'd had the nerve to take her to task for being ten minutes late arriving for work.

When she had reminded him this was her family's estate agency that had been set up by her grandfather and who did he think he was, he had calmly informed her it was now his agency and if she didn't intend getting to work on time, she had better find another job.

★　★　★

'Hello Anna. Problem?'

Lost in her thoughts, Anna hadn't noticed a car draw up behind her.

'Hugh.' She greeted Archie Wainwright's son with a beaming smile. 'Just the man I need.'

'You do look in a bit of a mess. What are you doing up here?'

'Hillcrest Farm is up for sale and Phil wanted me to do a preliminary survey. The owners have apparently had the property on the books of another agency for ages, but with no luck.'

Hugh nodded. 'I'd heard the owners were selling up and moving to Australia to be with their daughter. But why on earth didn't you drive up?' He looked down at her feet. The hems of her once smart trouser suit were damp and stained. 'And why didn't you wear a pair of boots?'

'Because I didn't want to carry them. And I'm walking because my car wouldn't start. My father gave me a lift to the bottom of the hill. I didn't realise it was quite so muddy up here.'

'You should have given me a call.'

Anna bit her lip. Much as she liked Hugh Wainwright, she was determined to keep their relationship platonic, which meant she couldn't go calling on him every time she was in trouble.

Her mobile rang, saving her from replying.

'Hello?'

It was Phil Anderson. 'Anna? Where are you?'

'Hillcrest Farm.'

'Not according to the owners you're not. They've rung in to complain that you're half an hour late.'

'My car wouldn't . . . '

'I don't want excuses, Anna. I want results. Hillcrest Farm is a significant property. It doesn't do to upset important clients. So just get on with your job!'

Two patches of pink rose to Anna's cheeks as Phil rang off. How dare he speak to her like that! And Hugh would have overheard every word.

'Come on,' Hugh said now, as he

leaned over and opened his passenger door. 'Jump in. I'll drive you the rest of the way.'

Inside his car it was cosy and warm and Anna sank into its depths and took a few moments to repair her hair and re-apply her lipstick. There was nothing she could do about her shoes, but at least her feet were dry now.

'How are you getting on with Phil Anderson?' Hugh asked. 'I wasn't eavesdropping, but he seems to be giving you a rough time.'

'Tell me about it,' Anna muttered, trying to remember the details of the property that the goat had so helpfully shredded.

'Of course it's none of my business,' Hugh put in, 'but if I can help in any way?'

'Thanks and all that, Hugh, but I can handle it.'

'Well, if ever you need a shoulder to cry on.'

Anna just nodded and said, 'You turn here.' She pointed to an ancient, weather-beaten sign.

'Nearly missed it.' Hugh swung the steering wheel round, and moments later they drew up outside a red-bricked farmhouse.

'It's a nice property, with a lot of land.' Hugh got out of the car and opened the passenger door for Anna. 'Would you like me to come back and collect you? I'd like to have a look round. I've never been up here before.'

'No thanks, Hugh, that's OK,' Anna told him. 'I'll phone for a taxi when I'm finished.'

'If you're sure?' Hugh glanced at his watch. 'I do have another appointment but I could always re-schedule.'

'I'm sure. And thank you.'

After one last look round, Hugh got back into his car. Anna watched him drive off, his red tail lights disappearing down the hill.

She turned her attention to the farmhouse to find the owner, Mrs Tindall, standing on the doorstep with her arms crossed and her lips pressed together in an expression of disapproval.

'So you've arrived then? Not before time.'

'Mrs Tindall? How do you do? I'm Anna Villiers.'

She found herself talking to Mrs Tindall's back.

Anna sighed. Why was life so difficult? She was doing her best but fate was throwing every obstacle it could think of in her way.

She followed Mrs Tindall's vast form down a gloomy corridor and into an equally gloomy kitchen.

'Hello Mr Tindall,' she greeted a gruff-looking man seated at the table, reading a newspaper.

He barely looked up to return her greeting.

★   ★   ★

It was late afternoon before Anna got back to the office. Her stomach was rumbling so loudly she was surprised Phil couldn't hear it. The farmer's wife hadn't even offered her so much as a cup of tea. She and her husband had left Anna to her measuring and note-taking while they'd sat down to aromatic bowls of thick vegetable soup and crusty bread.

'Phil's out,' Sally, the receptionist, informed her, adding, 'you'd better freshen up before he gets back. He's not in a good mood.'

'Neither am I.' Anna slapped her notes down on to the desk.

'Mrs Tindall?' Sally enquired sympathetically.

'Do you know her?'

'I know of her. I've heard she drives a hard bargain. She's the sort of client who's very hard to please.'

'Don't I know it.' Anna grabbed her emergency sponge bag out of the bottom drawer of her desk and headed for the washroom.

She almost shrieked with fright at her reflection in the mirror. Her sleek bob looked like a bird had nested in it. The cutting wind had made her eyes water and mascara had trickled down her face, giving her the appearance of a careworn clown, and somehow she had managed to get marker pen on the collar of her crisp white blouse.

Repairing the damage as best as she could, she went back to her office.

'Want a cup of tea, Sally?' she called through to Reception, 'and a piece of cake? I think there's some coffee gateau left over from yesterday.' There was no reply from the outer office. 'Sally? Are you there?' She poked her head round the door. Sally's chair was empty, but standing by her desk was the imposing figure of Phil Anderson. He had Anna's notes in his hand.

'Er — hello. I've just got back,' Anna said.

His eyes worked up from her damp trouser bottoms to the blue splodge that she had been unable to totally remove from her blouse. 'So I see.'

His voice wasn't warm, it wasn't cold, it wasn't anything. Nonetheless, it made Anna gulp nervously. And when she was nervous, she tended to gabble.

'A fine job that was.' She tried a smile that didn't really work. 'You should have gone up there. I don't think Mrs Tindall liked me and she didn't offer any refreshment. I think her husband might have done but she rules the roost, I can tell you. I pity their poor daughter. She probably moved to Australia to get away from them. Would you like a cup of tea? I'm gasping for one.'

'What I would like,' Phil said, 'is an explanation.'

'Of what?'

'We are here to do a professional job. We are not in the business to criticise our clients, or to inconvenience them.'

'Inconvenience them?' Anna echoed with a puzzled frown.

'I've had Mrs Tindall on the telephone complaining you were late arriving and overstayed your welcome.'

'I told you, my car wouldn't start.'

'According to Mrs Tindall, you arrived in a car driven by a man.'

Anna blinked. 'Well, yes. Hugh

Wainwright . . . '

'Hugh Wainwright?' Phil snapped. 'What was he doing up there?'

'He was passing by and offered me a lift.'

'Passing by?' Phil shot her an incredulous look. 'No-one passes by Hillcrest Farm unless they have business up there.'

Anna frowned. Now she came to think about it, that was a bit strange.

'Hugh Wainwright's father is a property developer,' Phil said.

'I know that.'

'And I suppose you are now going to tell me that you didn't know about Archie Wainwright being after Hillcrest Farm, too?'

Anna's head began to spin. 'Why should he be after Hillcrest Farm?'

'It's a very desirable property and he's been trying to get his hands on the land for years. He probably sent his son up there to sniff around.'

'What for?' Anna frowned.

'He wants to pull down the farmhouse and build on the land.'

'But it's miles from anywhere.'

'That won't matter to the sort of people who would buy his properties. They're looking for privacy and are willing to pay for it. It has beautiful views over the estuary and easy access from London. It's an ideal place for building second homes, and that would rip the heart out of the local community. But now, thanks to you, it looks very much as though Archie Wainwright has got a foot in the door.'

'But Hugh didn't stay. He only . . . '

'You've got five minutes to leave the premises.'

Anna gasped as the full meaning of Phil's words sunk in.

'But . . . are you firing me? You can't do that.'

'I just did.'

'But . . . '

Phil turned on his heel, and without a further word he stormed into his office and shut the door.

Anna's Father Has A Suggestion

'Hello, darling. You're home early. Got the sack?' Anna's father greeted her with a kiss.

'Yes.'

Her father's smile froze on his lips.

'I was only joking,' he said in astonishment.

'I wasn't. Phil Anderson has fired me, Dad.'

'You're not serious.' Her father still didn't look convinced.

'I am.' Anna threw her coat onto the sofa, 'and if you're having a drink, I'll join you.'

She watched her father fill two tumblers then carry them over to join her on the sofa.

'What happened, Annie?'

Her father only ever called her Annie

when he knew she was upset.

'Have you heard of Hillcrest Farm?'

George Villiers frowned. 'The Tindalls' place? I'd heard they were selling up. It was the sort of property I always had my eye on, but it didn't come on the market in my time.'

'It's on the market now.'

'So what's the problem?'

'Phil Anderson sent me out there to do a survey.'

'You didn't tell me.'

'Client confidentiality, Dad, you know that!'

'But it's a long walk from the bottom of the hill. I could have taken you.'

'Dad, you were already late for work because of me.'

They both know Anna's flat battery wasn't the only reason her father had been later for work. Filling shelves and stocktaking at the local supermarket was hardly comparable with having run Villiers Properties and Estates, now known as Anderson Villiers, for over twenty years. Much as Anna loved her

14

father, she knew he had not inherited her grandfather's business flair, and in the space of eighteen months they had seen their business dwindle in the face of stiff competition in a shrinking market.

For a while it had seemed the agency would fold and they would be forced into selling Mallards, the house that had been in their family for generations, but then Phil Anderson had come to their rescue. Anderson's was a newer, brighter, modern agency that was doing well, but needed the reputation of an agency like Villiers to increase its turnover.

Anna's father had struck a deal whereby they would merge and he would stand down from the agency on the understanding his daughter kept her job.

'You needn't lose out, Annie, because of me.' He had explained the situation to her over dinner the night before the merger went through.

'But you can't leave, Dad,' Anna had

protested, 'you're the backbone of the agency.'

'There isn't room for me in the new set up, Annie, and one of us has to go. It can't be Phil Anderson, so that only leaves me.'

That had been six months ago and, from their very first day of working together, Phil Anderson seemed to take against Anna. Nothing she ever did was right.

For her part, she he had been too proud to tell Phil that the reason for her frequent lateness at work was due to her very ancient car needing a complete overhaul, something she could not afford.

'To cut a long story short,' Anna said now, 'Archie Wainwright is after the land surrounding Hillcrest Farm and Phil thinks I'm in cahoots with him.'

'What?' George Villiers exploded. 'Why would he think that?'

'Hugh gave me a lift up to the farm. Phil found out about it and,' Anna shrugged, 'that's it, in a nutshell.'

16

'You mean he fired you without giving you a chance to explain?'

'That about sums it up.'

'He can't do that.'

'He can and he did. He's the boss. What he says goes.'

'We'll take him to a tribunal. He can't get away with this. It's outrageous.'

Anna shook her head. She was beginning to feel fuzzy. She'd eaten nothing since a snatched piece of toast at breakfast.

'No.' She put out a hand and clutched her father's arm. 'There's nothing we can do. We haven't got the backing to take on the likes of Phil Anderson, and he knows it. He's been looking for an excuse to get rid of me for ages and today I provided him with the perfect one.'

'It's all my fault, Anna.'

'Now you're talking nonsense, Dad. And in a way, Phil's right,' Anna admitted grudgingly. 'I should have been at the farm on time and I have been late getting into work recently.

'So what's for supper? I'm famished.'

'Have it your own way, Annie, but I'm not happy about this.'

'Dad? Food?'

George sighed, knowing that once his strong-willed daughter had made up her mind, nothing would change it He kissed her forehead. 'How does smoked salmon, scrambled eggs and brown bread and butter sound?'

'Fantastic. Where would I be without you?' She smiled into her father's tired eyes.

'You don't know how good it makes me feel to hear you say that, Annie,' he said gently. 'Now, why don't you go and soak away the worries of the day in a hot bath while I see to supper?'

★ ★ ★

'So, what are you going to do?' George brewed up some coffee after they'd finished washing up.

'I don't know,' Anna admitted. 'The

only thing I can do is sell houses, and I can't even do that now, it seems.'

'But there's your degree,' her father protested, 'that must stand for something.'

'An honours degree in the history of art doesn't really get you very far in the business world, Dad, and while I may know the difference between cubism and impressionism, it wouldn't get me a job in a supermarket.'

They sat down opposite each other at the scrubbed pine table.

'Why don't you ask Hugh Wainright to help? I'm sure his father could offer you something.'

'No way. What more proof would Phil Anderson need to prove his point?'

'Would you like me to have a word with him?'

'Who?'

'Phil Anderson.'

'No, Dad. I know you mean well, but it's time I stood on my own two feet. I've still got some of Grandfather's money and I can live on that for a while. Something's bound to turn up.'

George Villiers bit his lip. In his opinion his daughter was being a tad optimistic. The supermarket job had only come his way after their first choice of applicant had decided not to accept the position.

★   ★   ★

Anna looked down at the marks on the old kitchen table. The stains on it had been made by years of family living. The first time she'd painted her nails then spilt varnish remover all over it had left a mark that nothing had been able to eradicate.

Grandfather had loved to build his little model aeroplanes in here and bits of glued-up newspaper were forever getting stuck to the table, much to the annoyance of Anna's grandmother.

Anna traced a cobalt blue paint stain with her forefinger. Her mother, too, had used this table for her arts and crafts.

Oh, how she missed them all.

'I had wondered,' her father cleared his throat, 'if you and Hugh were . . . ' he left the sentence unfinished.

'I like Hugh, Dad, but there's nothing between us.'

'You were childhood sweethearts.'

'More like brother and sister, really, and it may have escaped your notice, but I've grown up now. It's not something I can put my finger on, Dad, but I know Hugh is not the man for me.'

'He is very much under his father's thumb,' George agreed, 'and I'm not sure I entirely trust Archie Wainwright. He's sailed close to the wind once or twice if the rumours are to be believed. A man like Phil Anderson would suit you better.'

Anna jerked herself up right. 'I cannot believe you said that.'

'Why not? He's built himself up from nothing. He's honest and hardworking.'

'And he ruined this family.'

'Anna, love, we were going downhill

long before Phil Anderson came on the scene.'

Anna stifled a yawn. 'Sorry, Dad. Much as I'd like to debate this issue with you, I'm having difficulty keeping my eyes open.'

'Why don't you go on up to bed? I'll see to Dixie then lock up down here.'

'Night, Dad. Night Dixie.' She kissed her father, cuddled the family spaniel, then made her way upstairs.

She was asleep before her head touched the pillow. At some time during the night she thought she heard the telephone ring and the sound of footsteps on the landing, but there was no knock on her door and she drifted back into a dreamless sleep.

A Dark Cloud On
The Horizon

Celeste Eden preferred to paint in the mornings. The sunlight slanting through the windows lit up her corner of the studio in Ash Park House, the Residential Centre where she lived. She took a deep breath as she inspected her previous day's sketches.

The commission had not been an easy one. Portraits were not one of her strengths and the subject had been difficult — the sulky child of a City magnate. However, Celeste had done her best and the initial draft somehow managed to disguise the pouting lips and scowling face of the troublesome teenager, whose mother had told Celeste she intended hanging the portrait in the main hall of their house. 'To welcome visitors,' she gushed.

Privately, Celeste thought that such a portrait would have repelled visitors, but such unprofessional comments she kept to herself.

Celeste's lips curved into a warm smile. The child had been called Grace and anybody less graceful she had yet to encounter. But, with her generosity of spirit, Celeste had felt sorry for the youngster. During the pre-sitting interview, by using her special brand of Celtic charm, Celeste had managed to draw the girl out of herself. Family life wasn't easy for the lumpy daughter of a beautiful, pushy mother and an ambitious father who was rarely home. It was no wonder the child resorted to tantrums to get attention. In her position, Celeste suspected she would have done exactly the same thing.

Andy, the warden of the Home came into the studio. 'I know you don't normally do this type of work, Celeste.' He hesitated, uncertain how to go on.

'But we need the money,' Celeste had finished what he had been about to say, 'and if I can churn out a reasonable portrait in an equally reasonable space of time, we could charge a premium rate.'

Andy's brow cleared. He didn't like doing this sort of thing any more than Celeste, but with costs rising, and the parlous state of the centre's finances, they needed every bit of income they could get.

'I knew you'd understand, Celeste,' Andy said.

One of the pleasures of his life was dealing with the lovely Celeste Eden. Life had dealt her a raw deal, yet he had never heard her complain. 'Do you think you can do it?' he asked her.

'Just give me the tools for the job.'

'Thanks.' He smiled at the beautiful woman busy cleaning her paintbrushes in preparation for her day's work. 'I don't know what we'd do without you.'

'I feel the same way about the centre, Andy. You've been my lifeline and I'll do anything to help.'

'You are extremely fashionable, you

know. Everyone wants a Celeste Eden to hang on their wall. The mayor was most impressed with that collage you did for the town hall.'

'Let's hope it leads to more commissions.' Celeste paused. 'You can tell me the truth, Andy. How are things, really?'

Andy shook his head. 'Same old story. I'll fight tooth and nail to save this centre, but we're just not paying our way. I've heard a rumour that Archie Wainwright's after our land and he is one powerful man with friends in all the right places.'

'But Ash Park House is part of the local community. It's a focus point and it's been here since Victorian times.' Celeste was appalled at what she was hearing.

'I don't think the Archie Wainwrights of this world care about that sort of thing. Ashton Vale has everything going for it — good train connections, lovely scenery, the soft Dorset countryside, it's not far from the sea and the winters are mild. What more do you want? The area is tailor-made for the young professional set, and Archie's set his sights on turning this place into a housing development. And you and I both know that he's ruthless when it comes to business dealings.'

'He won't get his hands on Ash Park House if I have anything to do with it,' Celeste said firmly.

'Still,' Andy smiled, 'we're not there yet. So I must get on. Sure you've got everything you need?'

'I'm fine, Andy. Thanks.'

'What's on the timetable today?'

'I've got an art class at ten. Then this afternoon I'm doing a talk at the youth centre.'

'And Grace's portrait?' Andy asked tentatively.

'I'll find a window,' Celeste assured him, privately wondering how she could cram another twelve hours of work into her busy day.

'If you need anything, ring your bell.'

'Will do.'

After Andy had gone, Celeste took a few moments to relax. She hadn't slept well in the night, but rather than be a nuisance to the staff, she'd tossed and turned, trying to get comfortable. Wet weather always made her joints ache, and although they were well into April, the rain showed no sign of easing up. What Celeste would really have liked to do was have a nap for half an hour or so to recharge her batteries. She straightened her shoulders, dismissing the luxury of such a weakness. A few stretching exercises were all that were needed to put things right.

A draft of air drew her attention to the door. She looked up and a smile of pleasure crossed her face as Jenny Barrow, the physiotherapist, walked into the studio.

'Just the lady I want to see. I'm feeling a bit of a crock this morning. Can you put me right?' Celeste said.

'I don't know where you get your

energy levels from. If I was half as much of a crock as you,' Jenny smiled, 'I'd count myself lucky.'

Jenny helped Celeste out of her wheelchair and on to the massage couch tucked away in another corner of the studio. She drew the curtains round the cubicle while Celeste settled herself down.

'You do too much,' she chided Celeste.

'I have to, Jenny. You know me. Never could sit still.'

'All the same, we don't want you having a setback.'

'Yes, miss.' Celeste tried to look meek, but failed miserably as an impish smile lit up her face. 'I've been toying with ideas for a project for my art students. What do you think about a new wall painting for the activities centre?'

'It's possible.'

'We need something bold, something to stir the imagination. Do you think any of the nurses would volunteer for a bit of modelling?'

Jenny's freckled face softened into laughter. 'I hope you're not thinking of anything too racy.'

'Well, I haven't put it out of my mind. Think of the fun we'd have doing it.'

'Honestly, Celeste,' Jenny began to work on her legs, 'sometimes you're outrageous.'

'But you wouldn't have me any other way, would you? Ouch.'

'Sorry. Did that hurt?'

'Bit tender.' Celeste bit her lip. 'Didn't sleep very well last night. So, how about you?'

'How about me what?'

'Modelling for the wall painting.'

'I will not dignify that suggestion with a reply,' Jenny said, trying not to smile. Much as she loved Celeste she didn't want her overdoing things and she knew from experience that with the slightest bit of encouragement that was exactly what she would do.

'Have you heard the rumours?'

Celeste asked, closing her eyes as Jenny's expert fingers worked their magic on her joints.

'About Archie Wainwright? Who hasn't? That man seems determined to rip the heart out of the local community. If he has his way, all the local cottages will be sold to incomers who will only visit at the weekends, and every bit of available land will be sold off and developed to within an inch of its life.'

'Sir Nigel would be turning in his grave.'

Sir Nigel Malmsby had been the Victorian industrialist who had set aside a large part of his land for the purpose of building the original Ash Park House. Although over the years the property had been renovated and extended, there had always been a residential therapy centre in Ashton Vale. The occupants, people like Celeste Eden, were encouraged to take as active a role in the community as was possible. As a result, Ash Park House had developed a fine reputation for nursing and pastoral care.

Lately, though, economic considerations had begun to bite into every aspect of its daily life, casting a question mark over its future. Andy Soames, the new warden, had been appointed to the post with the remit of raising the profile of Ash Park House. The Board of Trustees of Sir Nigel's legacy had given him a twelve-month deadline, after which time, the situation would be reviewed.

★　★　★

'There.' Jenny finished massaging Celeste's legs. 'Feel better?'

'Much,' Celeste replied.

'Don't forget your exercises when you get a spare moment.'

'I won't.'

'How's that daughter of yours getting on, by the way?' Jenny asked, as she packed up her equipment.

'She's coming to visit me at lunch-time. I can't wait. It's ages since I've seen her. She leads such a busy life.'

'And you don't, I suppose?' Jenny raised an eyebrow at Celeste. 'Now, remember what I said. If you feel tired, ease up.'

'I'll try,' Celeste promised, 'but I've got so much to do, it won't be easy.'

'Why do I feel I'm banging my head against a brick wall?'

'You're not. I listen to every word you say and I promise I'll follow your instructions to the letter.'

'Letter,' Jenny slapped the pocket of her uniform. 'That reminds me. Reception asked me to give you this. It came in the post this morning.' She passed over an official-looking envelope. 'Now remember, no questionable paintings in the activities centre. The sewing club would be all of a flutter.'

Celeste opened her letter after Jenny had gone. It was from Phil Anderson, wanting to arrange a meeting with her. She frowned. Why would he want to pay her a visit? She sighed and put the letter to one side. No doubt she would get around to replying to it in time.

Hugh Wainright
Visits Anna

'If things go on like this I may be reduced to joining you, Dad.' Anna joked, as she hung up on another fruitless call.

'I don't want you working in the supermarket,' George Villiers said with an unhappy frown.

'Well, Grandfather's money won't last for ever and it's been over a week now without even the sniff of an interview.' Anna scratched her head with her pen. 'How can you be over-qualified for a job?'

'Because, my darling, you are a brilliant girl and if you'd only let me speak to Phil Anderson on your behalf, I'm sure we could sort something out. All this sacking business is just a silly misunderstanding.'

'We've already been down that road, Dad. He fired me, so he's hardly likely to re-employ me.'

'But if he knew the full facts?'

'His answer would still be no.' Anna pushed her hair back, revealing the hairline scar on her forehead.

It wasn't an unsightly scar and George always longed to tell his daughter there was no need to use her fringe to disguise the evidence of her childhood accident, but he knew any comment of that nature would have entirely the reverse effect on Anna.

Outwardly she presented a confident, focused image, but George knew it hid an insecurity brought about by her ambition to prove herself on her own merit. Being born the granddaughter of Robert Villiers, her path through life should have been an easy one, but ever since her mother's horse-riding accident, when Anna had been only five years old, her life had been far from easy.

The loss of her grandmother a few

years after her mother's accident had resulted in Anna being sent away to boarding school at an early age. And without the glue of his wife's wisdom and care holding the family together, Anna's grandfather began to lose his grasp on the family business. Several deals slipped through his fingers and while his son George had done his best to keep the agency viable, he had not inherited his father's flair for business and things had begun to sink into a gradual decline.

'In the old days I would have been able to call in favours from any number of contacts who would have been falling over themselves to offer you a job,' George said with a shake of his head, 'but not now.'

'I don't need you to call in any favours on my behalf, Dad. I can stand on my own two feet,' Anna said firmly. 'Times are tough, but it won't be the first time we've had to weather a storm.' She smiled fondly at her father across the kitchen table. 'I'm optimistic. Look, there are loads of ads in the newspaper.'

George stood up and put on his jacket. 'I'd better be going. I'm due at work. Would you like me to leave you the car while the garage is seeing to yours?'

'Certainly not. You'll be tired when you finish your shift, and it's a long walk to and from the supermarket. If I feel like a breath of fresh air later, I'll take Dixie out for a walk.'

There were dark circles under her father's eyes, the cause of which, Anna suspected, was one too many sleepless nights. He worked long hours and Anna was sure he blamed himself for the downfall of the family fortunes.

'Tell you what.' She smiled brightly at him. 'See if you can snaffle any more of that smoked salmon for supper. I'm sure there's a bottle of decent wine hidden away somewhere. What say we make a party of it?'

Her father's tired face lit up. 'Good idea.'

★   ★   ★

Anna listened to her father drive off down the gravelled driveway. Despite what she had told him, she wasn't that confident about finding work, at least not in the near future.

She turned her attention back to the situations vacant column. What exactly was an Outreach Co-ordinator? she thought, as she circled the advertisement and picked up the telephone.

Rain slapped against the kitchen window, and Dixie barked from her basket by the boiler. Although it was the last week of April, the light wasn't that bright and Anna had been squinting at the newspaper for hours. Her eyes felt sore and she had the beginnings of a headache. Her temples were throbbing as she pushed the paper aside.

'Sorry, Dixie,' she threw her pen down on the table, 'forgot the time. You'd like a walk, wouldn't you?' She glanced at the clock. 'I'll make myself a coffee, then how about we both do Ash Wood?'

Her suggestion was met with the thud of a happy tail. Anna stroked the spaniel's soft golden hair. The lick of Dixie's warm tongue against her fingers was reassuring. Some things never changed.

Dixie had been her last birthday present from her grandfather. She and Anna had grown up together and it was to Dixie Anna had turned when life had seemed way beyond miserable and, in her turn, Dixie had limped towards Anna the day she'd trodden on a piece of glass in the wood and cut her paw.

She barked now, as Anna was filling the kettle with water. Moments later the front doorbell rang.

'Clever girl. Where would I be without my trusty guard dog?' Anna patted Dixie's head and made her way down the hall. Mindful of the fact that she was alone in the house and that Mallards was a remote property, she secured the chain across the door before opening it.

'Anna, is that you?'

'Hugh.' She undid the chain. 'What are you doing here?'

'Thought I'd call by, see how you were.' He smiled his charming smile.

Anna opened the door. 'I was about to make some coffee.'

'You know me. Never say no to a shot of caffeine.' He followed her into the kitchen. 'So, how's tricks?' He settled down at the table while Anna sorted out two mugs.

'Not too good,' Anna admitted.

'I'd heard about you and Phil Anderson parting company. I'm sorry, Anna. Was it my fault he fired you? Because if so, I'm willing to explain everything to him.'

'Not you as well,' Anna protested. 'I can fight my own battles, you know.'

'The offer was well meant,' Hugh said.

'And that was rude of me. I'm sorry, Hugh. I didn't mean to be short with you, but first my father, and now you. Everyone wants to have a word with Phil Anderson on my behalf and honestly, while I'm very grateful, I really don't want that kind of help. If there's any crawling to be done, I'll do it myself, and even then, I'd have to be desperate.'

'But Sally, his receptionist, said he didn't let you explain.'

'When were you talking to Sally?'

'I bumped into her the other day as she was leaving work. She told me what happened. She thinks it's unfair, too, and quite frankly, she's on the verge of giving in her notice. Ever since you left, she's been unable to cope.'

'Filing never was her strong point,' Anna agreed with a smile, remembering the number of times she had bailed out their lovely but scatty receptionist. 'But tell her not to do anything foolish on my account. Good jobs aren't easy to come by and, well, Sally's not the most efficient,' Anna finished.

'Talking about new jobs, have you given any further thought to my father's offer?' Hugh said.

Anna shook her head. Although she

and Hugh weren't an item, they had gone out together from time to time, mainly to make up a foursome or to attend a business function. On nearly every occasion she had bumped into Hugh's father. It had taken all Anna's diplomatic skills to turn down Mr Wainwright's frequent job offers. The name Villiers still carried a certain cachet in Ashton Vale and Anna suspected it was for this reason alone Archie Wainwright was keen to have her on board.

She passed Hugh his mug of coffee then sat down opposite him.

The newspaper was still on the table. Hugh looked at the jobs she had circled. 'Local Government?' A look of disbelief crossed his face. 'That's not for you, Anna. All that form filling would drive you mad.'

'Maybe so. But I've got to keep trying. Bills have to be paid.'

'Why don't you take up Dad's offer?' Hugh persisted. 'Who knows,' he leaned forward, 'we may even turn a professional relationship into a personal one.'

'We're going over old ground here, Hugh.' Anna was trying to let him down as nicely as she could, but she wished he would realise they had no future together.

'As you wish. Just remember, the offer's still there should you ever need it.'

'Thanks, Hugh.' Impulsively she patted his hand. 'A lot of our so-called friends disappeared when the family's fortunes took a turn for the worse. I hope I can always call you my friend.'

'You know I'd like to be more than that, Anna.'

She backed away from Hugh immediately. 'OK.' He smiled reluctantly. 'Subject closed. Friends it is.'

Dixie began barking again. 'I promised her a walk,' Anna said.

Hugh downed the last of his coffee and stood up. 'In that case I'll take my leave. I can find my own way out. Don't forget, I'm only a phone call away if you need me.'

★ ★ ★

Anna breathed a sigh of relief as she heard Hugh close the front door behind him. She rinsed out their mugs and left them to dry on the draining board.

Seeing Anna unhook her lead off the wall, Dixie began barking in earnest. Anna clipped the lead to her collar.

'Come on then, Dixie, I think we both need to clear away a few cobwebs. We'd better go out the front door. Make sure Hugh really did close it behind him and check that he's not lurking in the bushes.'

Still barking with excitement, Dixie's paws pattered down the corridor as Anna opened the front door. And came face to face with Phil Anderson.

A Surprising Turn
Of Events

'Goodness, you startled me.' Anna stepped back in surprise, narrowly missing landing on Dixie.

'Sorry. Were you going out?' Phil's brown eyes took in her dog walking coat and the panting Dixie straining at the leash. He was dressed casually in jeans and a jumper. A rather beat up 4 × 4 was parked on the forecourt behind him. Anna was always surprised he didn't drive a top of the range sports job, rather like Hugh's state-of-the-art Italian number.

The first time Phil had driven up to Mallards for a meeting with her father, she'd thought he had come to cut down the trees, and had directed him round to the back of the house. Phil's cutting correction of her misunderstanding still made her cheeks burn. She would have apologised for her mistake, but her father had arrived on the scene and the moment had passed.

Later, Anna realised the 4 × 4 was a practical choice of vehicle, as Phil was often called out to remote properties situated miles down rutted and muddy tracks.

At the time of the merger, she had intended asking Phil for a new company car to replace her trusty, but ageing, hatchback, but her courage had failed her. Now she was glad she hadn't been granted a company car, which she would have had to hand back. An ageing car was better than no transport at all, and living at Mallards without a car was not an option.

'I could come back if it's not convenient,' Phil said.

'No. Um, my father's out.'

'It's you I've come to see.'

'Oh, Right. Well, are you up for a walk? Ash Wood? Dixie hasn't been out all day and we could both do with a breath of fresh air.'

'Fine by me.' He inspected the sky. 'I'll get my waterproof from the car. It looks like more rain.'

Anna watched him stride back to the four track. The anorak he retrieved from the back seat was as muddy as the car. Somehow, in casual gear, he didn't look quite so intimidating, and she wondered what it was he had to say to her. She locked the front door and popped the key in her pocket.

'Ready?' Phil was back at her side.

'There's a short cut to the wood round the back of the kitchen garden.'

'Kitchen garden? That sounds very grand.' Phil raised an eyebrow, stinging Anna into retorting, 'We still call it that even though it's years since it supplied any kitchen staff with fruit and vegetables.'

'Of course,' he said, with the merest twitch of his lips. To her annoyance, Anna knew she was blushing. 'Should I have used the tradesmen's entrance?' he said.

'There isn't one,' she snapped, her blush deepening at the reference to her past faux pas, then bit her lip as his smile deepened and she realised he was joking.

*   *   *

Anna had a habit of saying the wrong thing when she was nervous, and right now she was more than nervous. She wanted to know what Phil Anderson was doing on her doorstep and why had had chosen to accompany her and Dixie on a walk, but pride prevented her from asking.

'I saw Hugh Wainwright driving away,' Phil said, as he slackened his pace to match hers.

'It was a social call. He came to see how I was.'

'And how are you?'

'Fine,' Anna replied airily.

Surely that couldn't be a note of concern in his voice?

She was beginning to wish she'd

worn a bit of make up to hide her scar. She never normally went out without foundation or a headscarf, but today she had done both. It would be the day Phil Anderson had chosen to visit, she thought with a rueful smile.

Deciding she may as well reveal the real reason for Hugh's visit, she said 'Actually, Hugh offered me a job.'

'Did you take it?'

Anna was surprised at the sharp note in Phil's voice. 'The offer's still open if I'm interested,' she said.

'You're not seriously thinking of going to work for Archie Wainwright?' Phil had stopped walking and Anna almost cannoned into him. Dixie let out a yelp of indignation as her collar tightened.

'Sorry, Dixie.' Anna knelt down to pat her. 'I'll let you off the lead as soon as we reach the meadow.' She straightened up. 'She has a habit of running after rabbits and once she ran out into the road, and narrowly missed being hit by a car.'

Aware that Phil was still looking at her expectantly, Anna played for time. 'Sorry, what was that you were saying?'

'The Wainwrights . . . are you going to work for them?'

'No.' Anna challenged his brown eyes with her blue ones. 'Despite your poor opinion of me, I do have some principles.'

They had begun walking again and had now reached the door in the wall that led out into the meadow behind the house. 'I am finding it difficult to get another job, but I expect you know that,' she added.

★ ★ ★

Once outside, she unclipped Dixie's lead and watched her race off into the undergrowth. Anna took a moment out to watch her go. The air smelt rain-washed and the scent of late spring lingered in the mist.

'The thought of Wainwrights getting their hands on all this,' she waved a hand in the direction of the meadow overlooking the distant wood, 'fills me with horror. I grew up here and the fields are a haven for wildlife. It's up to us to protect it.'

'I agree with you,' Phil said.

Anna blinked raindrops off her eyelashes. It was now raining steadily, and the day matched her mood.

* * *

'Do you want to turn back?' Phil asked, as they made for shelter under a tree.

'Turn back?' Anna repeated in amazement. 'You can if you like, but I've walked these fields in far worse weather than this.'

'Me too. Not these fields,' he added. 'I used to walk a lot when I was younger, just to get out of the house. I love my sister to bits, but when she was in a mood, it was best to make yourself scarce and in her teens she was one moody girl. We all used to scatter.'

Anna cast him a sideways glance,

51

waiting for him to say more. When he didn't, she said, 'In that case, shall we walk on?'

'Fine by me.'

Unable to contain her curiosity any longer, Anna asked, 'So why are you here? The reason for your visit?' she prompted.

It was a few moments before Phil replied. 'Actually, I was wondering if you would like your job back.'

Anna stumbled and Phil put a hand under her elbow to steady her.

She managed to gasp, 'Would you mind repeating that?'

'I'm offering you your old job back.'

'Why?'

'Sally's given in her notice. Her boyfriend's got a job in France and she's going out there to join him.'

'So, in the space of a few weeks you've managed to lose your receptionist and the Villiers of Anderson Villiers?' Anna raised an eyebrow at Phil. 'Nice work.'

'I've come here to try to put things

right between us,' Phil responded stiffly.

'By asking me to take over Sally's job?'

'No. But it would help if you could do some receptionist duties until we get a replacement.'

'I see.'

'You know everybody in Ashton Vale and to be honest, lots of people have asked where you are. I can't run the office on my own and I'm prepared to admit I might have been a bit hasty in dismissing you. I wasn't aware of the facts.'

'You didn't ask for them. In fact, you wouldn't let me tell you, if I remember rightly.'

'I have apologised.'

'Have you? Admitting you've been a bit hasty isn't my idea of an apology.'

'Look, I'm here to make amends, Anna. If you are interested, the job is yours again.'

'This hasn't got anything to do with my father, has it?' Anna asked suspiciously.

'No. Why?'

'He hasn't been to see you?'

'Why should he?'

'He wasn't best pleased over what happened between us and he wanted me to take my case to a tribunal.'

'I'm glad you didn't,' Phil admitted. 'That sort of thing is very damaging to a business.'

'Even if I'd wanted to, I couldn't afford it,' Anna said. 'But it didn't stop me being furious. You didn't give me a chance to explain what had happened. And you must know Mrs Tindall isn't the easiest person in the world to deal with.'

'I realise that now. I'm sorry.'

Anna felt a small glimmer of respect for Phil Anderson. It took a lot of courage to apologise and admit you were in the wrong.

'Shall we say it was case of six of one and half a dozen of the other?' she suggested, prepared to meet him half way.

'Agreed,' Phil said, a look of relief

crossing his face. 'Do you need time to think about my offer?'

'No, but we need to get a few things straight before I accept.'

'Fair enough.'

'I just want to point out that I am not working behind your back with the Wainwrights. Hugh and his father are family friends. Hugh was very kind to me when,' Anna paused, 'when I was young. I know his father has plans for Ashton Vale, but I don't know any of the details and they do not include me.'

'I realise that now. Before Sally left, she put me right on one or two things.'

'Sally's left already?'

Phil had the grace to look shamefaced. 'I'm afraid I wasn't entirely truthful with you just now.'

'You mean she hasn't gone to France with her boyfriend?'

'That bit was true, but she didn't give in her notice. She walked out after she told me in no uncertain terms exactly what she thought of me. She made me realise that I might have been a bit, well, a bit harsh on you.'

'So, who's manning the office now?' Anna asked.

'No-one. All calls are on divert and I had to shut up shop before coming out to see you. Of course, we'll need to advertise for a new receptionist, but in the meantime, if you wouldn't mind sharing the duties with me, I would be very grateful.'

Anna glanced at her watch. 'You'd better get back. Early evening's usually a busy time and you don't want to leave the office unmanned for too long.'

Phil looked at her hopefully. 'You haven't given me your answer.'

'And I'm not going to right now.'

'Anna, I don't have time to play games. I have to know. And I don't need you to let me down gently if that's what's worrying you.'

Anna took a deep breath. 'What I suggest is that you offer me a three months' trial, a sort of probationary period, in case either of us has second thoughts.'

'I don't think . . . '

'You may have changed your mind about me, but I haven't completely changed mine about you. You pre-judged me without asking for my side of the story. You didn't give me a chance to explain. That's not how things are done in my book. There has to be mutual trust and respect.' Anna straightened her shoulders. 'Three months, at the end of which time either of us can terminate the contract.'

There was a flicker of reluctant respect in Phil's brown eyes. 'You're more like your grandfather than I gave you credit for,' he said.

'So do we have a deal?'

'We have a deal.'

Anna held out her hand and Phil shook it firmly.

'I'll be with you first thing in the morning. Can you find your own way back?'

Without waiting for his reply, she strode off calling out for Dixie, who had disappeared in the direction of Ash Wood.

Celeste Learns More About Phil

Phil Anderson smiled down at Celeste Eden. 'You got my letter?'

'A week ago. I'm sorry I wasn't able to see you before now, but I've been very busy. I run art classes and I've had several commissions to complete. Please, sit down.' Celeste motioned to a chair. 'Now, what is this all about? I'm intrigued.'

Phil frowned as he sat down opposite Celeste. 'Have we met before, Ms Eden? You look familiar somehow,' he said.

'It's Celeste, and no, I don't believe so. Perhaps you read the piece the Gazette ran a week or so ago? It wasn't a very good picture, but they did a good write-up on Ash Park House.'

'That must be it,' Phil agreed. 'Now, the reason I'm here is because I've been approached by Andy Soames.'

'The warden? He didn't mention anything about it to me.'

'We were just playing around with a few fund-raising ideas. As you know the financial situation regarding Ash Park isn't too good.'

'That's why I'm working a twenty-four-hour day. Andy's had some great ideas, but it all adds to my workload.'

'That's what I told him. You work a punishing schedule and I think it's unfair to ask you to do any more.'

'You know my trouble, Phil?' Celeste laughed lightly. 'I've never been able to say no. Am I right in guessing that Andy suggested we meet up because he's had another brilliant fund-raising idea?'

'Something along those lines, yes,' Phil admitted. 'But I'm reluctant to place a further burden on your shoulders.'

'Don't worry about me, I'm as strong as an ox.' Celeste slapped the armrest of her wheelchair. 'My painting has nothing to do with my legs. Stick me in front of an easel and canvas and I could stay there forever.'

'So, what's Andy's latest idea?'

'We were thinking of putting one of your paintings up for auction to raise funds for the centre.'

'Good idea. But where do you come into things?'

'It's my intention to place a reserve on the painting.'

'Meaning?'

'People bid for what they think your painting's worth and I match their offer.'

'Whatever the final selling price is, it's automatically doubled. Does that make sense?'

'You mean, even if the bids are low, we still get some money?'

'That's exactly it.'

'Sounds a good deal to me,' Celeste said, then added, 'but why would you do this for us?'

Phil hesitated, then said, 'It's difficult to know where to start.'

'I always find the beginning's a good

place. Look, do you want some tea? Have a look round while I make it. Nothing's out of bounds, but don't touch anything, the paint might not be dry.'

★　★　★

Celeste's studio was an Aladdin's Cave of pictures. Phil frowned as he lifted the worksheet off a pile of stacked canvases in one corner of the room.

'Isn't that Mallards?' he called to her.

'Yes, it is,' Celeste said. 'Know it, do you?'

'George Villiers' house? Yes, I've been there. I work with his daughter, Anna.'

'Yes, I know. She's a lovely girl.' Celeste looked up from stirring the tea. 'It was such a shame when things went wrong for the family, but Anna's a bright girl, so make good use of her.'

'We didn't exactly get off on the right footing.'

'Hardly surprising, is it? Villiers Properties and Estates was set up by

Robert Villiers years ago. It can't have been easy for Anna watching you come in and take over what by rights should have been hers.'

'I see you know all about me,' Phil said.

'I know you're thirty years old and a veritable whiz kid. It said so in the Gazette.' Celeste balanced the tea tray on her chair and moved carefully back to the coffee table. 'No, don't help me,' she said briskly. 'I don't need it. But thank you,' she added with a smile.

She busied herself pouring milk and tea into the cups then nudged a plate of biscuits towards Phil.

'Thanks, I missed lunch.' He bit into a custard cream and chewed thoughtfully for a few moments. 'Are you very friendly with the Villiers family, Celeste?' he said.

'Why do you ask?'

'I've encountered quite a bit of local hostility recently. I have to admit I brought a lot of it on myself when I fired Anna Villiers.'

'I'm not surprised. Anna's well liked in Ashton Vale. They don't know you. You'd immediately be cast as the bad guy.'

'I realise that now. And I lost a good receptionist because of my hasty actions. The thing is, you may share those opinions. I wouldn't blame you if you did, and you may feel you don't want to work with me. So I'll understand if you turn me down.'

'I'm sure Anna gave a good as she got when you fired her,' Celeste said with a wry smile. 'Old Robert Villiers wasn't above telling people exactly what he thought of them and Anna's inherited some of his traits. And no, I won't turn you down. Ash Park means too much to me to let personal issues stand in the way of business.'

'You think it's a good idea, then?'

'To hold an auction here? Yes I do. Of course we would have to adapt the studio, I've got a lot of clutter that would need clearing out. Still, one thing we're never short of here is volunteers.'

'We need to fine tune the details, but Andy's got lots of ideas.'

'I'm sure he has. And anything to stop Archie Wainwright getting his hands on this land.' Celeste sipped her tea. 'But you still haven't told me your reason for wanting to help out. I mean, it's obvious why I want to do it, but you're not even local, are you?'

Phil shook his head. 'I was brought up in Bath.'

'I thought I recognised the accent,' Celeste smiled. 'I used to spend a lot of time there before my accident. I fell off a horse, in case you were wondering. I don't tell everyone, but if we're going to work together it's as well you should know. Now it's your turn. Tell me about yourself.'

★　★　★

There was something about Celeste Eden that fascinated Phil. He couldn't put his finger on it, but he still couldn't shake off the feeling that they had met somewhere before, despite her denial.

'Only the bits you want me to know, of course,' she added with a smile.

Phil leaned back in his chair. 'I was brought up in Bath, but I wasn't born there. I was born in Scotland.'

'That explains the rich chestnut hair. Sorry,' Celeste said, 'that's the painter in me coming out.'

'So go on. Why did you move south?'

'I was adopted,' Phil said.

'Sure you want to go on with this?' Celeste said gently. 'I wouldn't want you to think I was prying.'

'It's no secret. I don't know my real mother, but I think, I hope, she must have been in desperate straits to give me up for adoption.'

'Any mother would be.' Celeste agreed, a look of sadness flitting across her face. 'To be parted from a child is a terrible thing.'

Phil looked down at Celeste's hands. She was wearing a wedding ring but she'd made no mention of a husband or family.

'My parents, my adoptive parents,' he went on, 'were marvellous people. I was very lucky. They treated me like their own son. My father was a vicar, a fine man. They thought they couldn't have children of their own, but when I was a year old, my mother found out she was expecting, so when my sister was born, we were the perfect family. They treated both of us exactly the same.'

'That sort of thing often happens, I believe. Are your parents still alive?'

'No. My only relatives are my sister and her family.'

'So why do you want to help us out at Ash Park?'

'I,' Phil cleared his throat, 'well, I went through a bit of a rough patch in my teens — nothing too serious. If it hadn't been for a therapy centre very much like this one, I might not have made it. Now I'm in the position of being able to put something back into this centre, it's what I want to do.'

'Right,' Celeste said briskly, 'that's enough personal history for me to be going along with and I like what I hear. Now, if you've finished your tea, we'd better discuss business.

'I need to know what form you'd like my painting to take. To be honest, I'm fed up doing commissioned portraits, I much prefer landscapes. Do you think a landscape would be appropriate?'

'More than appropriate. Do you have any ideas?'

Celeste nodded. 'Many years ago I spent a happy time in Italy. Our hotel overlooked a beautiful lake. I've never seen anything like it. We used to go on to the balcony at sunset and watch the water change colour as the sun slid from the sky. I can still remember every ripple in the lake.' Celeste smiled. 'I really can, you know. I can remember every detail of that holiday because it was one of the happiest times in my life.'

A short silence fell between them. Phil sensed there was perhaps more Celeste wanted to say, but she didn't.

'Right, fine,' he said. 'I'll have a word

with Andy, then, if that's all right with you?'

'What sort of time frame are we talking about?'

'A month?'

'Six weeks. I like my paintings to dry properly and I don't want to be rushed.'

'Then six weeks it is.'

Hugh Tries To Influence Anna

The lights from the trees in the garden were reflected in the Olympic-sized swimming pool. Anna watched the guests stroll through the gardens and into the restaurant towards the sumptuous buffet laid out on a long table at the far end of the room.

'You haven't been listening to a word I've said,' Hugh complained.

Anna turned her attention back to her companion with an apologetic smile. Her thoughts had been miles away from the stuffy ballroom. During her earlier walk with Dixie, she had been entranced by a carpet of bluebells in the woods. The sight had filled Anna with a renewed determination that earth movers must never be allowed to destroy Ash Meadow and turn it into another soulless housing estate.

'Sorry, Hugh. I was enjoying the twilight. It's such a beautiful evening,' she said.

'The first of many, I hope.' Hugh poured himself another glass of wine. 'Sure you won't have any?'

'Not for me.' Anna shook her head. 'I've just got my car back on the road and I don't want to do anything silly.'

'Why you didn't let me drive you here tonight is beyond me,' Hugh complained.

'I like to be in the office early in the morning and that means early nights. I don't want to give Phil Anderson another chance to fire me.'

Hugh nodded in reluctant agreement. In a far corner of the room his father was busy networking with important clients. No expense had been spared in hosting this evening. Hugh would be required to do his bit later, but for the moment he was free to sit with Anna.

'Sound her out, my boy,' his father had advised him. 'Now she's back working for that Anderson fellow, she may be a useful contact. Always as well to know what the opposition's up to.'

★　★　★

'I'm sorry you didn't take up Dad's offer of a job,' Hugh said to Anna, 'but it's understandable, really. There should always be a Villiers working for your company.

'Still, it must have been a wrench losing the family firm to an outsider.'

'Officially, it was a merger,' Anna pointed out.

'Of course,' Hugh agreed. 'So, how's it going?'

'Working with Phil? It's early days. I've only been back two weeks, and without a proper receptionist things have been a bit hectic.'

But Anna had to admit she was enjoying Phil's fresh approach. Much as she loved her father, his business practices had been firmly based on those of her grandfather and Villiers had not moved with the times. Under Phil's guidance, they were venturing into new territory that Anna found exciting and stimulating.

'I understand your boss managed to sweet talk the Tindalls into placing Hillcrest Farm with you,' Hugh said.

Anna nodded, not sure exactly how much Hugh knew. Archie Wainwright had been after the property and it was to Phil's credit that he had been able to persuade Mrs Tindall that Anderson Villiers were the best people to deal with the sale after Anna's initial disastrous interview with the clients.

'The old man wasn't best pleased about Hillcrest Farm,' Hugh admitted.

'I can imagine.' Anna was unable to hide a smile, remembering how she had danced a jig in the office when she'd found out the good news.

'What on earth do you think you're doing?' Phil had said, as he emerged from the kitchen to find Anna pirouetting round the front office.

'Sorry.' She stopped mid-twirl. 'I

thought you were out.'

Phil's lips had twitched. 'So I see. May I know the reason for this unseemly behaviour?'

Anna flapped a letter at him. 'Mrs Tindall. We've got it! Her agreement! She wants us to act for her.'

'In that case,' Phil had said, 'perhaps you'd do an extra twirl for me. I've got two left feet when it comes to dancing.'

After that, any tension between them had eased, and Anna found herself looking forward to the challenges of the day, not dreading them as she had done in the past.

* * *

Hugh nodded to acquaintances as he talked to Anna — all influential contacts, she couldn't help noticing. She was sure she had spied a councillor or two with their wives, as well as the mayor, and the upwardly mobile manager of the new marina.

Anna couldn't shake off the suspicion

that she was being used. When Hugh had suggested a meal out, she had accepted his invitation. If nothing else, she felt she needed to explain why she hadn't taken up his offer of a position with Wainwright's.

'I thought your invite was for a quiet dinner, just the two of us,' she said to Hugh now. 'I had no idea it was to be a formal function.'

'Dad suggested I invite you, sound you out, as it were.'

Anna frowned. 'Sound me out. Hugh, what's going on?'

'Nothing.' He shook his head. 'No need to look so worried. The people here tonight are business contacts of my father. He's setting up a sort of bank of people who might be interested in his new project, if he ever gets it off the ground.'

'What new project?'

'It's all very hush hush at the moment, but the development plans . . . '

'I shouldn't be here.' Anna grabbed her bag and pushed back her chair.

'No.' Hugh grabbed her wrist. 'Don't go. I haven't finished explaining what this is all about.'

'I don't think I want to hear.' Anna lowered her voice, aware that she and Hugh were attracting one or two curious glances.

'Does Phil know you're here tonight?' Hugh asked.

'Of course he doesn't.'

'Then perhaps you should tell him before he finds out for himself.'

Anna blinked, sensing she was a pawn in some dangerous game. So far, things had been going well with Phil, but she was aware that one false move on her part could have disastrous consequences. She remembered the relief in her father's eyes when she'd told him Phil had offered her job back. She couldn't afford to lose it again.

Hugh still had hold of her wrist. 'Phil may have won with Hillcrest Farm, Anna, but believe me, when it comes to the crunch, he's no match for Archie Wainwright.'

Anna had always discounted the rumours that Archie Wainwright wasn't above influencing local planning decisions with a few well-chosen donations but Hugh was right about one thing. His father was a clever man and she imagined he would be a formidable opponent.

'I think you underestimate Phil,' she retaliated.

Hugh shook his head. 'He's no-one, Anna. Who are his people? What is his background?'

'His background isn't important.'

'It is when you're dealing with such high stakes and you're not a local. I mean, let's face it, he's no more than a working class lad who's made good.'

'There's nothing wrong with that.' Anna could feel her anger rising. 'So what if he wasn't born with a silver spoon in his mouth? And the same thing could be said about your father,' Anna pointed out, 'and he's not local either.'

'He's lived here for years.'

Anna bit down another retort. She longed to point out that Archie Wainwright may have lived in Ashton Vale for years, but may people still regarded him with suspicion.

'Phil Anderson got his degree from a business studies night school and worked on building sites and in burger bars to get the money to put himself through college,' Hugh said sneeringly.

This was news to Anna, but she didn't doubt its authenticity. Archie Wainwright would have run the fullest check on Phil's credentials. There wouldn't be an area of Phil's life that he did not know about.

'Whereas you were born into a comfortable family.' Anna could hold back no longer. 'Your father paid for you to go to an expensive private school, where you obtained how many GCSEs?' A slow flush began to work its way up Hugh's neck. 'You had to go on a crammer to get better grades, and even then you only managed to scrape . . . '

'That's not fair,' Hugh protested.

'You started this conversation, Hugh. And I would say Phil has more than proved himself. He's worked hard, and at the age of thirty, he's head of his own prestigious agency. Your father is now worried about the competition. Need I say more?'

'It's obvious on which side your loyalties lie.'

'Would you expect anything else?'

'I had hoped you'd understand our position.

'It's not as if we're doing anything behind your back.'

'If my father was still head of Villiers Properties, would you be talking about him like this?'

'Of course not.'

'Why not? My family's acumen wasn't enough to keep the business afloat. Without Phil's assistance, we would have gone under.'

'Why are you sticking up for him? You don't even like the man.'

'I — admire him, I admire what he's done.'

Anna could feel her blood racing. Hugh was looking at her as though he could not believe what he was hearing. Anna could hardly believe her words herself. Until now, she hadn't given a moment's thought to Phil's background or his business abilities. But to hear Hugh run him down made her feel somehow protective towards him.

'Did you admire him when he accused you of working against him?' Hugh said.

'That was due to a misunderstanding.'

'He didn't give you a chance to explain.'

'Look, Hugh, this conversation is going nowhere. If you've nothing else to say, I think I'd better be going. Thank you for this evening.'

'I do have something else to say.'

Anna sighed. She was beginning to feel tired. No matter how early she arrived in the office, Phil was always there before her. This morning had been no exception. Early starts were all very well, but coupled with busy receptionist duties and working late and going out in the evening, something had to give, and right now, all Anna wanted to do was to go home and go to bed.

'Can it wait?' she said to Hugh.

Hugh cast a glance over his shoulder. 'What Dad was wondering about is if you would be interested in doing a little, shall we say, unofficial work for us?'

'I'm not sure I follow you.'

'He feels it was a smart move of yours getting Phil to re-employ you.'

'I didn't. We both accepted that we'd been hasty and we came to an agreement.'

'Which suited him.'

'We've already been through all this, Hugh.'

'We could make it worth your while to report back to us any little, shall we say, interesting bits of information that may come your way.'

'Are you asking me to spy on Phil? To

be a paid snooper?'

'I wouldn't put it quite like that,' Hugh objected. 'I'm sure if the position were reversed, Phil would be making the same suggestion to you.'

Anna stood up. 'I don't think he would. And if he did, my answer to him would be exactly the same.'

'So you won't do it?'

'You can tell your father I am not interested in any of his underhand schemes. Now, if you'll excuse me, I really do have to go home. My father likes to wait up for me and it's late.'

'Mr Wainwright, Miss Villiers?'

They both turned. 'Smile please, for the Gazette.'

The next moment a flash bulb went off, and before Anna could object, the photographer had disappeared into the crowd.

Remembering Past Times

'We shouldn't be doing this.' Celeste smiled, as George Villiers eased himself onto the rug spread out on the lawn.

'Surely you've got time for a picnic lunch in the garden?' he said.

'I don't normally do lunch,' Celeste told him. 'My workload doesn't leave me much time.'

'You mustn't let Andy push you so hard.' George frowned in concern. 'We don't want you having a relapse.'

'I wouldn't do it if I didn't enjoy it, George. I've never been one for sitting still, you know that.'

'All the same, you mustn't overdo things.'

He smiled affectionately at the raven-haired woman opposite him. She was dressed casually in one of her work shirts and paint-smeared slacks. The scarlet scarf round her neck created a vivid splash of colour against her pale skin. There was the faint smell turps. It was a scent that always reminded him of Celeste.

The early May sunshine was warm on his back. It promised to be a lovely day. In the distance he could hear the drone of a lawnmower and the scent of newly-cut grass lingered on the air. Being with Celeste was easy. They enjoyed each other's company and didn't have to make an effort to fill the silences that fell between them.

George flipped open the lid of a wickerwork picnic basket. 'If you won't ease up on your schedule, then you must let me build you up. You always were too thin.' He laid a tablecloth on the grass and began sorting out plates and paper napkins. 'Now, a little ham and some Mediterranean vegetables for you, I think, with a generous splodge of potato salad. There, now eat up every bit.'

He piled up Celeste's plate and passed it over together with a hunk of farmhouse bread and a generous wedge of Normandy Camembert. 'There are some advantages to working in the local supermarket. I managed to persuade the supervisor on the delicatessen to give me stuffed vine leaves and some cherry tomatoes, too — I know they're your favourites.'

'Mm. Delicious.' Celeste dipped into her potato salad. 'You always did throw a good picnic, George, and this one reminds me of the Villa Santa Helena. We had all our meals al fresco there. Do you remember?'

George leaned back against a tree. 'I think,' he said quietly, 'that was the happiest time of my life.'

'We were both young and beautiful in those days. No,' Celeste held up her hunk of bread and waved it at George, 'don't say it.'

'Say what?' He affected a look of innocence.

'That I'm still beautiful now.'

'All right then,' George smiled slowly. 'I won't. But you can't stop me thinking it. And I wouldn't have you any other way — my beautiful Celeste,' he said softly.

'I thought Anna was the love of your life,' Celeste teased him.

'I love the pair of you and Anna is very like you in character. She's got the scar to prove it. If she hadn't been trying to climb over that wall into the kitchen garden as a child, she wouldn't have fallen and knocked her head and needed six stitches.'

'We both bear the scars of our foolishness,' Celeste said quietly. Then added, 'How is she getting along now she's back working for Phil Anderson?'

'Fine, I think. I hardly see her these days. She's gone before me in the morning and not back until late. We've taken to leaving each other notes on the kitchen table.'

'You know I've been commissioned by Mr Anderson, Phil, to do a painting for him? It was another of Andy's ideas. He wants to auction it off to raise funds for Ash Park with Phil putting up a matching reserve.'

'Good idea. But it's still a sad business. Who would have thought Ash Park would be reduced to such things?' George clenched his fist. 'Archie Wainwright is a menace. He's got to be stopped. I wish I could do something to help. The trouble is, Archie's a powerful man and he's got friends in all the right places.'

'That might be his downfall.' Celeste finished her salad and put her plate down on the grass. 'He might overreach himself,' she said.

'This land was willed to the Trust. He can't just walk in and take it over,' George said.

'He doesn't have to. If we don't raise enough money, we're going to have to sell off some of the land, anyway. Archie Wainwright only needs to bide his time and the land will just fall into his lap.'

'It mustn't be allowed to happen.'

'That's why Andy came up with the idea of a painting.'

'And it's a fine idea. People will pay

good money to have a Celeste Eden hanging on their wall,' George said. 'Have you had any thoughts on the subject matter?'

'I've decided to paint the lake at the Villa St Helena.'

George's eyes widened. 'Have you indeed?'

'You don't mind?'

'Not at all.'

'It meant so much to me and I feel I can put my heart into it.'

'Do you need my help? I've got some photographs in an album somewhere. They're a bit faded now, but I could look them out if you like.'

'Thank you, George. My memory might need a little jogging in certain areas.' An impish smile lit up Celeste's face. 'But I do remember the afternoon we took that donkey ride up to the monastery on the hill.'

'Tell me about it.' George raised his eyes. 'I'll never forget it. I almost had to get off and push mine. The wretched thing dug its hooves in and wouldn't move. It kept braying at me, and all I could see was the back of your mount disappearing into the distance. I don't know what I would have done if the thing hadn't suddenly decided to move. Trouble was, it then got it into its head to gallop to catch up with you and I had to cling on for dear life. It did my dignity no good at all, I can tell you.'

Celeste laughed with him at the memory. 'My poor George. Riding never was one of your skills.'

'That wasn't riding. It was an extreme form of human torture. I think that shepherd had it in for me because he took a shine to you. He gave me the worst-tempered animal he could find. If it hadn't caught up with you in that lemon grove, who knows what would have happened.'

'Felipe had beautiful brown eyes, now you come to mention it,' Celeste mused, 'and a lovely singing voice. He was only serenading me.'

George scowled at her. 'Any more of

that sort of talk and I may withdraw my permission for you to paint that lake.'

'Sorry, George, but you're the only person I can tease. You treat me like everybody else.

'When you're in a wheelchair, people think they have to treat you like a piece of porcelain china. Well I'm not that vulnerable, and I think that's why I'm always trying to prove myself.'

'You don't have to prove yourself to me, darling Celeste, and your paintings are proof enough of your talent.' George paused and then went on, 'but you will always be different from everyone else. And I'm not talking about your wheelchair. It must be something to do with your Celtic ancestry. It makes you stand out from the crowd.'

Celeste leaned forward and took his hand. 'Half an hour in your company, George, and I always feel better. Now, I really should be getting back to work.'

'Already?'

'I'm giving an art lesson this

afternoon, and before that, Jenny Barrow's booked in to give me a half hour massage. Sitting painting in one position for a long time stiffens my joints.'

'Well, if I can't make you stay, then I can't.' With a sigh George began clearing away their picnic. 'I'll try to persuade Anna to join us next week.'

'She'll come when she's ready,' Celeste said, 'but don't push her. And from what you say, it sounds like Phil's giving her a hard time.'

'Anna's having to cover for Sally, and I don't think Phil Anderson makes any concessions.' He sighed. 'None of this would have happened if I'd inherited my father's business brain.'

'Stop blaming yourself, George,' Celeste said briskly. 'Now, if I hold the picnic basket, will you take me back to the studio? I keep getting stuck in the soft grass and Andy gets annoyed when I carve up his beautifully mown lawn.'

As George leaned forward to take off

the chair's brake, Celeste raised a hand to his face and kissed his cheek.

'I do love you,' she said quietly.

'I know,' he replied, looking in to her eyes. 'And I love you too.'

An Old Friend of Phil's Disturbs Anna

'You're late.' Phil was manning the reception desk, his long legs stuck out in front of him. Anna nearly fell over them as she staggered into the office with her briefcase and files.

'I was working on the Tindalls Farm contract at home until midnight.' She stifled a yawn as she put her paperwork down on the desk. 'I e-mailed you my report. Haven't you read it yet?'

'I haven't done anything yet. Where on earth did Sally keep her appointments book? And what was her wretched password? I can't get into the computer and the telephone hasn't stopped ringing since I got in.'

Anna shrugged off her tailored jacket, straightened the cuffs of her crisp white blouse and deposited her briefcase on her desk. 'Shall we start again? Good morning, Phil,' she said calmly, 'how are you today?'

His lips twitched in reluctant acknowledgement of her greeting. 'Good morning, Anna,' he returned. 'And I'm fine. Sorry. I didn't mean to be so short with you.' He ran a harassed hand through his thick hair. 'Running a front desk is not one of my strengths. The sooner we get a replacement for Sally, the better.'

'The advert should be in the local paper today. And you could set up your own password for Sally's system,' Anna suggested.

'I thought the new person could do that. They'll be bound to have their own ideas.'

The telephone began ringing again. 'You answer that,' Anna said, 'while I log on.'

She made a few efficient taps on the keyboard and moments later the system was up and running. Leaving Phil to his phone call, Anna headed for the kitchenette and flicked the switch on the kettle jug.

Moments later, she returned with two mugs of coffee and placed one on Phil's desk.

'Thank you. Sorry I barked at you.' He took a grateful sip. 'Blame Mrs Tindall.'

'What's she done now?'

'The wretched woman's got herself involved in a boundary dispute. It seems she wasn't entirely honest with us regarding their land. I'll have to go up there again, unless you'd rather do it?' Phil asked hopefully.

'No way,' Anna said firmly. 'I'd only make the situation worse. Besides, the last time I went up there you fired me.'

★ ★ ★

Anna flicked open the Tindalls' file. 'According to my figures, the boundary of the farm stretches from Bishop's Wood to the east and Ash Park House to the west,' she said to Phil.

'That's what I thought,' Phil said. 'But apparently there's a ransom strip of land that runs right through the middle of the property. Mrs Tindall claims she didn't know about it. It belongs to her husband's brother, apparently.'

'She didn't tell us any of this. And there's no mention of it in any of the paperwork for the farm.'

'Her husband and his brother haven't spoken to each other for years, mainly because the brother lives abroad. Apparently, the property originally belonged to their father. Mr Tindall senior entailed it equally to both of his sons.'

'Son number one, our Mr Tindall, wanted to buy his brother out, except he couldn't afford all the asking price.'

'That's why a little bit of the land remained in his brother's possession.'

'Why didn't he take a corner of the property instead of a strip of land through the middle?'

Phil shrugged. 'Who knows? But it's

going to be a headache, that's for sure.'

'And I presume this brother has found out about the farm being put on the market?' Anna said.

'Yes. I believe he's back in this country, and when he found out what his brother was up to, he contacted him. He's got us over a barrel. We can't sell up without his agreement, but if he hasn't spoken to his brother for years, things aren't looking too good.'

'It sounds horrendously complicated.'

'That's families for you. I don't have to tell you what could happen if Archie Wainwright gets to hear of this.'

'We can't keep it quiet for long,' Anna pointed out. 'He may even know about it already.'

'That's why I've got to arrange a meeting with the Tindalls. Do you know anything about a brother?'

Anna shook her head. 'I could try asking my father, but he's at work and they don't like him taking personal calls.'

'The sooner I speak to this brother the better, but I'm not holding out much hope. When will your father be home?'

'I don't know. I could try leaving a message on his mobile. He may pick it up during his break.'

Phil nodded. 'Do that. Meanwhile, I'll check the deeds. There may be something in them about all this, although I doubt it.'

⋆　⋆　⋆

Anna retrieved the day's post from the letterbox together with a copy of the Gazette.

'You haven't got time to read the paper,' Phil said. Outraged, she opened her mouth to protest, then realised he was smiling at her. She turned her attention back to the situations vacant column, annoyed with herself for wanting to smile back.

She was glad she had insisted on the three-month clause in her contract. If the workload carried on at this rate, she would be renegotiating a pay deal at the first available opportunity. Phil's new ideas were all very well, but they created a lot of work, and right now, all resources were stretched to the limit.

'Here it is,' Anna folded back the newspaper. 'Our advert.' She tapped the display with her finger. 'Hopefully we'll get some response.'

'That reminds me.' Phil held up a Post-It note. 'A Valerie Masters called. Says she's an old friend of mine.'

Anna looked up, puzzled. 'Do I need to know that?'

'Blowed if I can remember her. Anyway, she'll be dropping by later to have an informal chat about the vacancy. Can I leave it to you? If she's any good, I suggest we take her on.'

'Don't you want to be involved in the selection process?'

'I trust your judgement.'

This time Anna did allow herself a smile of acknowledgement. Replacing Sally would be a hard task, but she knew exactly the sort of person she was looking for. Someone who could be as loyal and discreet as her predecessor and who wasn't afraid of hard work and, if she were female, wouldn't go falling in love with the boss.

Anna felt herself redden. Why on earth had that idea crept into her head? She wondered about this Valerie Masters. Exactly how old a friend of Phil's was she?

'By the way,' Phil said, 'talking about boundaries, that remind me. Ash Park House.'

'What about it?'

'I've arranged for Anderson Villiers to sponsor a painting in order to raise funds. An artist called Celeste Eden lives there, apparently.'

Anna's arm slipped off her desk, spilling coffee over the Gazette. She tried to pat it dry. It wasn't easy. Her hands were shaking.

'Have you heard of her?' Phil said, noticing her reaction.

'Everyone's heard of Celeste Eden.'

'Well, I went to see her last week. She's agreed to do a specially commissioned artwork for auction. Andy Soames will be the project coordinator.'

'I see.'

'It's as well you should know about it in case there are any telephone calls. All this is highly confidential, of course. We don't want Archie Wainwright getting wind of our plans.'

'You can trust me not to tell him, or his son,' Anna told Phil, 'but it won't be easy keeping our involvement quiet.'

'It's as well to be aware of how important this is. Hugh Wainwright . . .'

'Is no concern of mine.' Anna's mobile bleeped before she could say any more. She hadn't heard from Hugh since their disastrous date at the country club, when she'd found herself sticking up for Phil Anderson.

Anna looked down at her text. 'My father says he'll be pleased to see you at lunchtime. He has a forty-five minute break at one o'clock.'

'Right.' Phil stood up. 'That gives me

time to go out to Hillcrest Farm. Can you hold the fort for me?'

Anna nodded. 'I need to update Sally's records and input some new data. That should keep me occupied until you get back.'

Phil hesitated by her desk. 'Perhaps you'd like to be involved in the Ash Park House project? With your degree in art, our local contacts and public relation skills, you'd probably be a lot better at it than me.'

Anna put a hand up to her scar, a knee jerk reaction to his suggestion. It was something she always did when she was stressed. 'You mean work with Celeste Eden?'

'I'll introduce you if you like. We'll talk about it later, shall we?'

Just then the main door flew open in a rush of air.

'Phil.' Phil spun round at the sound of the female voice. A stunning blonde woman stood in the doorway. 'Lovely to see you again.'

'Who . . . '

'Valerie Masters?' Before he could move, she kissed him on both cheeks, laughing at his surprise. 'Valerie Wood to you.'

'Good heavens.' Phil's smile of confusion cleared as he returned her smile. 'What on earth are you doing in Ashton Vale?'

'It's a long story. I won't bore you with the details, but I need a job like, yesterday, and I understand you're looking for an assistant?'

Anna cleared her throat.

'Sorry.' Phil had a silly smile on his face as he turned back to her. 'Anna, this is a very old friend of mine, Valerie Wood, I mean, Masters. Valerie, this is Anna Villiers, my partner.'

Anna raised an eyebrow. 'Personal or professional?'

'Strictly professional,' Anna said firmly.

'I'm pleased to hear it.'

'I'm sure the two of you will get on together like a house on fire,' Phil said.

'I'm sure we will,' Valerie agreed and

held her hand out to Anna. 'If you'd like me to, I can start right now.'

She eyed the filing that was threatening to topple off the cabinet. 'It looks like I haven't arrived a moment too soon.'

'There may be other applicants,' Anna hedged, not wanting to be manipulated into a situation she might regret.

'We haven't had any so far,' Phil said, 'and we need someone desperately. It would save you a lot of trouble, Anna, what with interviewing and taking up references. You've better things to do with your time.'

'I've got references with me, in my handbag,' Valerie said eagerly. 'I admit I haven't worked for a while, but I'm sure if you telephoned them my referees would vouch for my good character. But of course, if Ms Villiers doesn't want me . . . '

Aware she had been wrong-footed, Anna was forced to smile at Valerie.

And she had to admit that employing

her now on a temporary basis would save a lot of time.

'I'm sure your references are fine.' She glanced at the letters Valerie had produced. 'We'll discuss terms later.'

'In that case,' Phil said, 'I must get on. Catch up with you later, Val.'

'Maybe we could have a drink one evening?'

'That would be nice.'

'I'll stay here until you get back, if you like. My time's my own these days.'

As Phil closed the door, Valerie turned to Anna. 'Now, Ms Villiers, where exactly would you like me to start?'

'It's Anna, and . . . '

A stack of filing chose that moment to slither off the window ledge onto the floor.

'I think,' Valerie said with a laugh, 'that answers my question.'

Moments later she was on her knees gathering up the sheets of paper strewn around the office. She scooped up the discarded copy of the Gazette and deposited everything on a spare desk.

'Perhaps you'd like to set up your password for the system?' Anna suggested.

'Right,' Valerie said. 'Of course. Password. Anything you say, Anna.'

Valerie Causes Trouble For Anna

'I don't know where I would be without you,' Celeste told Jenny, the physiotherapist.

'I wish all my patients were like you.' Jenny smiled. 'Most of them have to be forced to take their exercise. I have to try to stop you. So, what's on the agenda today?'

'I must get down to work on The Italian Lake painting. Recently, I've had so many demands on my time, I haven't made any real progress.'

'May I take a look?'

'Be my guest.' Celeste indicated a covered easel. 'It's that one over there. Only the bare outlines so far. What do you think of it?'

Jenny pulled off the cloth covering the canvas and stared at it for a long moment.

'Don't you like it?' Celeste asked anxiously.

'I think,' Jenny blinked, 'it's the most marvellous piece of work you've ever done. You've caught the light, and the tranquillity of the sunset, and the shading is absolutely perfect.'

Jenny leant forward. 'What's this little sketch here in the corner?'

'It's a joke really, a sort of human touch. It's a donkey.'

'Of course it is. Is there a story behind it?'

There was, but it was information Celeste did not intend sharing with anyone.

★ ★ ★

'There's no story really,' she told Jenny. 'I just wanted to add a light touch, a bit of fun.'

'That's the thing about your work, Celeste. It's fresh, vibrant and original. I know this sounds silly, but your work breathes.'

Celeste flushed with pleasure. 'That's one of the nicest things anyone has ever said about my paintings.'

'Is it an actual place, The Italian Lake?'

'It's very special to me and yes, it does exist.'

Instinctively, Jenny knew not to ask any more questions. It would border on prying and that was the last thing she wanted to do. 'Right, I'll leave you to get on then. Have a nice day.' Jenny picked up her bag, waved and almost bumped into Andy Soames who was coming into the studio.

'Can I have a moment of your time, Celeste?' he said with a worried frown.

'More problems?'

'You could say that.'

'What is it today?'

'I've just had a telephone call from the bank. They're getting a bit twitchy about the state of our finances.'

'There's nothing new in that.'

'They're talking about time limits now, repayments, that sort of thing. I've got a meeting with them and The Trust next week.' Andy paused. 'As you know, Archie Wainwright has put in a tentative offer for the land surrounding Ash Park.'

'You're not thinking of taking him up on his offer?' Celeste was aghast.

'I may have no choice. It's the last thing I want to do, but we can't carry on with things the way they are. The bank has been very accommodating so far, but they can't extend our lending forever and we now need even more funding.'

'Isn't that why we're holding the Open Day Auction?'

'It was, but now I doubt if we'll be ready in time to raise the money.'

'Not even if I work day and night?'

'I'm not having that,' Andy frowned. 'As it is, I'm worried you're working too hard.'

'Don't mind me.' Celeste smiled. 'I always was a workhorse.'

'May I remind you Ash Park is a therapy centre. Admittedly we encourage our residents to lead as full and productive a life as possible, but it's not our intention to work them into the ground.'

Celeste's light laughter greeted his words. 'We have a wonderful life here, Andy. We're spoilt silly. The activities centre does a wonderful job playing to people's strengths. If it hadn't been for the occupational therapist telling me I really could paint and to stop playing at it, and then buying me some equipment and telling me to get on with it instead of feeling sorry for myself, I wouldn't be where I am now. So no, I've no intention of easing up.'

'And actually, I have a bit of news for you. I haven't told anyone yet as it's all hush hush, but, given the circumstances, there's no time like the present.'

Celeste ferreted under a pile of paperwork. 'Where did I put it? Ah, yes. Here it is.'

She held a sheet of paper out to Andy.

'What is it?'

'Read it.'

Andy took the letter and cast his eye quickly down the page. He looked at Celeste. 'Is this for real?'

'I must admit I thought it was a joke to begin with.'

'Have you rung this Damian Chancellor back?'

'Yes. I spoke to his assistant and he is for real. He's an artist's agent. It seems someone showed him one of my paintings and he was impressed with it, so if we can work out a deal, he would like to represent me.'

'He's promised to come down for the auction, then he can take a proper look at my work, and if we like each other, we'll take it from there.'

'That's wonderful news, Celeste. I couldn't be more pleased.'

'Can you keep it to yourself for the moment, Andy? Only I've one or two ideas up my sleeve.'

'I may be able to talk Damian Chancellor into some kind of credit arrangement or sponsorship, or something along those lines, but I'm not too good on figures. I need to talk to Phil Anderson about it.'

Andy nodded. 'Good idea. I won't tell a soul, but if you do need any help, just let me know.'

'Thank you, Andy. Now, I'd best be getting on. Have you set a date for the auction?'

'I was thinking about June, if that's convenient for you? We thought people could look around at the work we do, have tea, that sort of thing, and then we could hold the auction in the activities centre.

'But will that give you enough time?'

'Perfect,' Celeste nodded. 'One or two of the helpers have agreed to help me price up my paintings. You never know, we may sell a few more at the Open Day.'

'Jenny's father was in sales many years ago before he moved abroad, but he's back on a visit and she's promised to bring him along for a bit of professional input, how to display the goods to their best advantage, sort of thing.'

'So, Andy, cheer up. All is not lost.'

'I suppose you wouldn't like a job running the business side of Ash Park?' Andy grinned.

'I once had a job in an office and I lasted one day, so thank you for your offer, but no thanks.

'Now off you go. I've a million things to do.'

★ ★ ★

After Andy had gone, Celeste picked up the telephone and dialled a familiar number.

'Anderson Villiers Properties.'

'Darling? Is that you?' Celeste said.

'Valerie speaking. Who's calling?'

'Oh. You're the new receptionist, are you?'

'I've been here a week now.'

'Celeste Eden here. Anna normally answers the telephone.'

'Anna isn't in the office right now, Ms Eden,' Valerie's voice was crisp and efficient. 'May I help you?'

'Is Mr Anderson there?'

'I'm holding all calls at the moment. Is it important?'

'Nothing that can't wait. Perhaps he could contact me when he's got a spare moment? It's Ash Park. He's got the number.'

Celeste replaced the receiver with a frown, then shook off her feeling of unease. Sometimes her Celtic sixth sense was a nuisance. There was absolutely no reason for her to mistrust Phil's new receptionist. After all, she had never even met the girl. All the same, she couldn't help feeling something wasn't right.

* * *

'Who was that on the telephone?' Phil asked, as she came into the front office.

'Celeste Eden.' Valerie quickly closed down her computer system.

'You should have put her through to me.'

'Sorry,' Valerie said with a smile. 'I

thought you didn't want to be disturbed.'

'I've always got time for Celeste.'

'Is Celeste Eden the artist who lives at Ash Park?'

'That's right. We're sponsoring an auction of her work, to help raise funds for the centre. Any idea what she wanted?'

'She said it wasn't important. Would you like me to call her back?'

'No, I'll drop by the centre. I need to talk to Celeste about Hillcrest Farm. When I had lunch with George Villiers, he told me a member of Ash Park staff was related to one of the Tindalls, so I'd like to have a word with whoever it is and perhaps get the inside story on the brother. Do you know where Anna is, by the way?'

'She hasn't been in all morning. I think she was going to work from home. She needed to back up those files from her laptop.'

'Hm. It was strange that work going missing. Still, we were lucky Anna kept copies on her laptop. If it hadn't been for that, I'd almost have suspected her of being the culprit, seeing as she was the last person to access the files. Get her on the phone for me, would you?'

'I tried ringing her earlier on, but there was no answer and her mobile's on voice mail.'

Phil frowned. 'What's she playing at? She knows we need to be in constant contact.'

Valerie hesitated. 'I don't know how close you are to Anna, Phil,' she began.

'In what way close?' Phil looked at Valerie suspiciously.

'Well, are you an item?'

'You know our relationship is purely professional.'

'Yes, of course. That's what I thought. I wouldn't have suggested anything else and I know it's none of my business . . . ' Valerie paused.

'But?' Phil prompted.

'I'm telling you this purely as an old friend.' She cast a half embarrassed look at Phil as if uncertain how to continue. 'I — I have heard a rumour about Anna and Hugh Wainwright.'

'They're childhood friends.'

'Did she tell you about Wainwright's offering her a job?'

'Yes. She turned it down.' Phil was now frowning. 'What are you suggesting, Valerie?'

'I'm not suggesting anything, but maybe she's still in contact with Hugh?'

'I don't think Hugh and Anna have been in contact for weeks.'

'Oh. Is that what she told you?'

Phil frowned. Had she? He couldn't remember. He might just have assumed there was no contact between the two of them.

'It's possible they've seen each other recently, I suppose. But what's this all about?'

'If those lost files got into the wrong hands,' Valerie said, 'well, they contained sensitive information, didn't they?'

'I'm convinced Anna was not involved in their loss. Now, if you've nothing further to say, I have to go.'

Valerie held up the crumpled office copy of the Gazette. It was still covered in stains from where Anna had spilt her coffee over it. 'Have you seen this? I found it on the floor when I was sorting out those files that fell over.'

Phil glanced at the newspaper, to where Valerie was pointing at a picture. It was of Hugh and Anna, seated at a table at the country club, holding hands.

Phil's knuckles tightened as he read the caption:

Hugh Wainwright and Anna Villiers, sealing a deal.

'Of course there may be an innocent explanation?' Valerie left the question hanging in the air, the tone of her voice implying that she couldn't think of one, 'but if that were the case, why hasn't Anna mentioned it?'

'I don't know.' Phil's voice was tight.

'It says here the party was held to drum up support for Archie Wainwright's new land development scheme.'

'I can see that.'

'Shall I keep trying Anna's number?' Valerie asked, her eyes alert as she watched Phil's reaction to the newspaper article.

'No. I need to talk to her personally. Phone me the moment she comes into the office. I'll be at Ash Park, with Celeste Eden.'

★ ★ ★

Outside in the car park Phil gunned his mud-spattered four track into life. How could he have been so wrong? He'd had a long chat with Anna's father over lunch and the picture he had painted of his daughter was far removed from the girl in the photograph holding hands with Hugh Wainwright.

'Unfortunately I did not inherit my father's business skills,' George had said with a smile, 'but Anna has. I know the two of you didn't exactly start off on the right foot. She was upset because of what happened to me, but that's all in the past now. Anna's honest and hard

119

working. I know the two of you will make the new agency a success. I'm so glad you gave her a second chance.'

And despite George's words, there was no way Phil could explain away the photograph of Anna and Hugh holding hands at Archie Wainwright's party.

They had to be working together. And if they were, it could mean only one thing.

Phil had been right in his suspicions all along. Anna was secretly working for Archie Wainwright.

An Astonishing Discovery For Jenny

'Hello, Dad.' Jenny Barrow kissed her father on the cheek. 'You're looking well. Happy Birthday for tomorrow.' She produced a brightly-wrapped present. 'No opening it beforehand.'

Jack smiled at his daughter. 'I hope you haven't wasted your money on anything expensive.'

Jenny laughed. 'I've just bought the children new school shoes, so you need have no worries on that score. My budget will only stretch so far.'

She looked round the elegant dining room of The Anchor Hotel. Their table commanded an excellent view of the sea-front. Expensive yachts were moored in the marina.

'Isn't this rather grand for us?' she said.

'It's my birthday and I get to choose the venue. Besides, I have some good news,' her father told her.

A waiter appeared at their table holding a tasselled menu.

'Let's order lunch first, then I'll tell you all about it,' Jenny's father said.

★ ★ ★

'So what's the big news?' Jenny asked as she scooped up the last of her delicious Pavlova.

Jack sipped his coffee. 'It's a long story.'

'What have you got up to this time?' Jenny smiled.

'Not what you think.'

'How do you know what I'm thinking?' she teased.

'Because you're my daughter and in some ways we're very alike.' He patted her hand.

'Are we?' Jenny wasn't convinced. They may have the same sandy hair and freckles, but that was as far as the resemblance went. Her father had travelled the world. Jenny had stayed put in Ashton Vale. She loved her job as Ash Park House physiotherapist, she loved the Dorset coast and, as far as she was concerned, there wasn't a better place on this earth to live. She had no wish to move.

'As you know, when your mother and I parted, I took myself off to South Africa,' her father was saying.

Jenny nodded. Apart from the occasional card and letter, she'd had very little contact with her father while she was growing up.

'I always did have a bit of wanderlust — never could stay in one place for long. I did all sorts of jobs and, for a while, I lost touch with my old life, as you know.'

★   ★   ★

When her father had contacted her again to say he was back home and wanted to meet up, Jenny had had conflicting emotions about the man who had, as she saw it, abandoned her when she needed him most.

But, she reasoned, he was back now, and, although she could never forget the past, she could accept that Jack was never cut out to be a conventional father. And she knew now that, all through her childhood and teenage years, no matter where in the world he had been, he had never stopped loving her.

'My brother and I fell out over your grandfather's will,' her father was saying now, 'so I made a new life for myself abroad. Your mother married again, you took her new name of Barrow, and I suppose your stepfather was more of a father to you than I ever was. I'm not making excuses for my behaviour.' He smiled at her. 'Only telling you how it was.'

'I understand,' Jenny said.

'Anyway, the years passed and I had a hankering to come home for a visit, see the old country again.'

'I'm glad you did.' Jenny squeezed his hand. 'Ever since Mum and Bob went to live in Spain, my girls have missed having a grandfather around.'

'That's why I now want to do my best for you all. You've worked hard and got yourself a good job as a physiotherapist, and I'm very proud of you, but life can't be easy as a single parent.'

'We manage,' Jenny said, twisting at her wedding ring round her finger. Malcolm's accident had happened when the children were still very young, and without her work and the kindness of people like Celeste Eden, she didn't know how she would have pulled through.

'Another reason for my visit home was that I'd heard from someone that your Uncle Samuel was putting Hill-crest Farm up for sale, so I needed to dig out my old papers. They were lodged with the family solicitor and we had a bit of a job finding the safety deposit box. It had been years since I looked inside it, but once I did, there it was, in black and white.'

Jenny's smile faltered. 'I'm not following you, Dad. There what was? And what's Hillcrest Farm to do with you? It belongs to Uncle Samuel.'

'Not all of it. I still own my little patch.'

'You own a bit of Hillcrest Farm?' Jenny repeated in amazement.

'A fact my brother seems to have overlooked.'

★　★　★

As families went, theirs weren't close. The two Tindall brothers had never really seen eye to eye and when Jack had moved abroad, all contact with Samuel and his wife had ceased. Jenny had exchanged the occasional Christmas card with them, but there had been no social contact for years.

'So Hillcrest Farm isn't Uncle Samuel's to sell?' Jenny said.

'Oh, he can sell his bit of it all right,

but not all of it. Of course, that fact may have slipped his mind. It's years since we did our deal. That wife of his wasn't on the scene at the time, and she may not even have known about it.'

'So what are you going to do? Sell out to Uncle Samuel?'

'No. I'm going to sell my plot to the highest bidder and, I have to admit, it's created quite a lot of interest from a certain party.'

Jenny stirred her coffee vigorously.

'Hey, steady on,' Jack laughed. 'You're spilling it into the saucer.'

'Sorry.' Jenny put down her spoon. The question she had to ask almost stuck in her throat. 'Who is this certain party?'

'A man called Archie Wainwright. I couldn't believe the price he was offering for such a small acreage.'

Jack tapped his pocket. 'But I've got the contract here to prove it. The money's all yours, Jenny. It's for you and the girls. I know it doesn't make up for not being around when you were growing up, but I hope it will make up for it now.'

★ ★ ★

Jack leaned back in his chair waiting for his daughter's reaction. The smile on his face turned to a frown when he saw her dismayed expression. 'Jenny, what's the matter? I thought you'd be pleased.'

'I am, Dad.' She hesitated. 'Only, I wish you hadn't done a deal with Archie Wainwright.'

'I don't understand.'

'You wouldn't know about it and I expect he took great care to see you didn't find out.'

'You've lost me here, Jenny.'

'Archie Wainwright is after all the spare land in the area. He's got plans for an exclusive development of houses. Hillcrest Farm is on a prime site. He's had his eye on it for ages.'

Jack was now listening intently. 'Go on,' he urged.

'You see what this means? Archie Wainwright owns that piece of land . . .'

'So Samuel will be able to sell the farm to him without any problem,' Jack finished for her.

'That's why we're having the Open Day at Ash Park, remember? To save the land. You're coming to help place the paintings for us.'

Jack smacked his forehead. 'I never connected the two. What a fool I've been. I should have suspected a rat. That Archie Wainwright was far too eager to get me to sign his contract. But I'm not too good when it comes to money matters. Sales has always been my game. Oh, Jenny love, I'm so sorry.'

'Dad,' Jenny gulped. 'I can't believe it. We've sold out to Archie Wainwright.'

'No, we haven't.' Jack banged the table. 'I'm not going through with the deal. I'm not having some developer carve up my childhood home to make millions for himself.'

'But, Dad, you can't back out now, there'll be all sorts of penalties. Archie

129

Wainwright's bound to have tied up the contract with all sorts of clauses and legal loopholes. It's the way he operates.'

A slow smile spread across Jack's sun-tanned features. 'One thing I learned in all my travels, Jenny, is, never sign a deal immediately. Sleep on it overnight, that's been my motto. I had my solicitor look at the paperwork for me, to make sure it was in order. He said it was, but I haven't actually signed it yet.'

He gave a half-embarrassed smile. 'I was going to make a little ceremony of it over lunch. Get a couple of the waiters to witness my signature in your presence.'

'You haven't signed the contract?' Jenny looked at her father with a glimmer of hope.

'And I'm not going to. I'm going to tear it up.'

'Can you do that?'

'Try stopping me,' Jack laughed.

'Aren't we getting in a bit deep?'

Jenny was beginning to feel worried. 'It doesn't do to tangle with Archie Wainwright.'

'It doesn't do to tangle with me, either. No, I've made up my mind. I'm not going to sell the land to anyone. I'm going to make it over to you.'

'But Uncle Samuel . . . '

'It's nothing to do with him. It's my property and I can do what I like with it.'

'But don't you need the money?'

'Jenny,' Jack said gently as he leaned forward and took her hands. 'I'll probably be off again in a few months. I've got my own little place outside Durban. What's the money or the land to me?'

'But you can't leave us again, Dad.'

'You know what I'm like,' Jack said, almost apologetically. 'But of course I'll keep in touch. These days it's much easier with e-mails and texts. And I want to see my grandchildren grow up. I'll rig you up a web cam before I leave.'

He smiled at his daughter. 'Don't

131

worry, I'm not going yet, and certainly not before your Open Day. But giving you title to my bit of land means you can do what you like with it. Samuel's not an unreasonable man. He might make you an offer. Or this Phil Anderson everyone's talking about might be interested in it. What's he like, by the way? Not another Archie Wainwright, is he?'

Jenny shook her head. 'I don't know him that well, but he's sponsoring Celeste's painting for the Open Day auction.'

'He sounds a good man. Look, you don't have to take my advice, Jenny, but if you're thinking of selling the land, I suggest you deal with him.'

'All this is a bit over my head, Dad,' Jenny confessed. 'I'm not a business-woman.'

'Then for the moment I suggest you don't do anything at all.'

'Do you think Archie Wainwright will make trouble?'

'No need to concern yourself with him.'

'Now, I'd like to see this Ash Park House of yours. When is the Open Day?'

'End of the month,' Jenny said in a distracted manner.

'What's wrong?' Jack said. 'Don't tell me Archie Wainwright's walked in?'

'No, but I'm sure that's his son, Hugh. No, don't look. There's a woman with him and I think I recognise her.'

'Who is she?'

'An old school friend of mine — Valerie Wood. She's Valerie Masters now. I'd heard she was back in Ashton Vale and working for Anderson Villiers.'

Jack whistled under his breath. 'The people handling the sale of Hillcrest Farm?'

'Exactly.'

'And she's having lunch with Hugh Wainwright?'

'Yes. And I've a feeling she's up to no good.'

'You know, I thought life in Ashton Vale was going to be dull,' Jack said. 'I couldn't have been more wrong.'

Celeste Has An Amazing Confession

'You.' Phil stopped mid-stride and stared at Anna. 'What are you doing here?'

During the ten-minute drive to Ash Park House, Phil had gone over all the plausible reasons as to why Anna should have been at Archie Wainwright's party.

He could come up with only one satisfactory answer. She had to be working for him.

And now, bumping into her in the foyer of Ash Park House when she was supposed to be working from home, confirmed his suspicions.

She was clearly here to try to find out about the auction.

* * *

Anna looked startled to see Phil as she emerged from Andy Soames' office. 'I could ask you what you're doing here,' she replied coolly.

'I'm here on business. I'm visiting Celeste Eden.'

'Why?'

'I think that's my affair, don't you?' He kept his voice cold, determined not to dwell on the porcelain quality of her skin, on the soft curves of her neck. What was the matter with him? The girl was nothing more than a double agent, yet here he was, his heart beating like a drum at the sight of her, when all she'd done was doublecross him from day one.

'And my business here is my affair, too,' Anna said. 'I do have a life away from Anderson Villiers, you know.'

'Correct me if I'm wrong, but weren't you supposed to be working from home today?'

'I was. I mean, I am,' Anna replied, looking flustered.

Phil raised his eyebrows. 'You live here?'

'No.'

'Valerie has been trying to contact you all morning. All she managed to raise was a voice mail message.'

'Mobiles aren't allowed at Ash Park. The sound waves can interfere with the equipment. I had to turn off my phone.'

'For heaven's sake, Anna, you are supposed to be in constant touch with the agency in case of any emergency, you know that.'

Anna bit her lip. 'Yes. I'm sorry. I wasn't thinking.'

There were dark circles under her eyes and she looked tired. Phil ignored any feelings of concern. She had every reason to look exhausted. Until now he'd assumed the long hours she put in at work were for the sole benefit of Anderson Villiers. His mouth tightened. He knew better now.

'You haven't answered my question,' he said sharply.

Anna ran a hand through her hair. Phil frowned. Her clothes looked as if she'd slept in them and he couldn't help noticing her fingers were stained with blue paint.

'I can't remember what your question was,' she admitted with a tired smile.

'I asked you what you're doing here.'

'And I can't tell you.' They were now attracting curious glances from residents and staff, so Anna suggested, 'Can we go outside? I could do with some fresh air. And I think we need to talk.'

Against his will, Phil found himself agreeing. He didn't want to talk things through with Anna. He didn't want to have to listen to another pack of lies, but all the same, he followed her down the corridor and out into the flower-bestrewn meadow surrounding the house.

The soft grass brushed against his trousers. Anna, he noticed, was wearing a skirt, a gentle pastel affair with a matching top, a change from the normal severe business suits she usually favoured.

She opened a small wicket gate that

led down to the wisteria-clad summer-house by the lake. The breeze blowing off the water was a refreshing relief.

'Are you a voluntary worker here?' Phil asked, hoping that was the reason he had bumped into her outside Andy's office.

'No. My reasons for being here are private.'

'As in Archie Wainwright private, I suppose?'

'What do you mean?' Anna turned to him with a puzzled frown.

'Well, you're certainly not here on Anderson Villiers business.'

'No. I . . . '

'Did you lose those files on purpose?'

'What files?' Anna blinked.

Phil frowned. 'The ones you're supposed to be retrieving.'

'Yes. Sorry. Um, I'm working on them.'

Phil decided to come right out with his suspicions.

'Have you been passing confidential information over to Hugh Wainwright?'

Anna looked shocked. 'No!' she protested. 'How could you even think that?'

'Because you're here, because . . . oh look, Anna you have to tell me what you're doing here. After all, you said you were too tied up on other projects to get involved in the Open Day Auction.'

'That was because . . . ' Anna bit her lip, as if she were uncertain how to continue.

'Because it would mean a conflict of interests?' Phil finished the sentence for her.

'Something like that,' Anna agreed, 'but not with Wainwrights. I don't have anything to do with them. You have to believe that.'

'Well, I don't. Valerie showed me the picture of you and Hugh Wainwright in the Gazette. You were holding hands and smiling for the camera.'

Anna closed her eyes and sank down on a wooden seat by the summerhouse. 'I was going to tell you about that.'

'Oh really? When? Or were you hoping I wouldn't find out?'

'No. I . . . ' Anna took a deep breath. 'Hugh asked me out for dinner. I thought it might be a good idea to accept his invitation and find out what his father was up to. It was only when I got to the country club that I realised his father had arranged a reception for people he thought might be interested in his new project. By then it was too late to back out.'

'I was about to leave when a freelance photographer took that picture. I didn't know it was going to be in this week's Gazette.'

'Why should I believe you?'

'Because it's the truth.'

'I'm beginning to think you're one of those people who has difficulty distinguishing truth from fiction.'

'That's not fair,' Anna retaliated.

'I've been more than fair with you, Anna. I've given you every chance to prove yourself. I've offered you a position in the new company, initially against my better judgement. I believed you when you said you hadn't seen Hugh Wainwright for weeks. Today, you're supposed to be working from home, backing up files that have inexplicably been deleted from the office system, yet I find you at Ash Park House and you won't tell me why you're here. All of this leads me to believe you're hiding something from me.'

'I'm sorry. I can't say any more.'

'Can't, or won't?'

'Both.'

Phil's attitude softened.

'Are you in some sort of trouble?' he asked. 'Is that it?'

A sad expression flitted across Anna's face. 'No more than usual,' she said.

Phil had a sudden desire to ease the lines of worry from her face. Despite evidence to the contrary, he still found it hard to believe she was two-timing him. 'Can't you share your problems with me?' he said gently.

Anna blinked the sun from her eyes

as she looked directly at Phil. 'I can share with you what I do know about Archie Wainwright. He has expressed an interesting buying up some of the land surrounding Ash Park and the Board of Trustees has given Andy Soames an ultimatum. If he doesn't come up with a viable business plan, Ash Park may have to be sold off to the highest bidder.'

'You're not telling me anything I don't already know. That's what the auction and the Open Day is all about — raising funds.'

'I know.'

'We seem to be going round in circles,' Phil said in exasperation. 'I'm trying to help you, but it's got to be a two-way thing, Anna. I'm also trying not to believe you'd join forces with Hugh and his father against Anderson Villiers.'

'I would never do anything to damage the reputation of Anderson Villiers! My grandfather was Robert Villiers. He founded the company.'

'Which by rights you should have inherited.'

Anna's eyes widened. 'And you think I'm on some sort of revenge trip?'

'I don't know what to think. But your father seems convinced you and I are the right team to carry Anderson Villiers through to the next generation.'

'I would have liked to do that,' Anna said, and stood up, 'but I don't think it will be possible.'

'Any relationship has to be built on trust — and you don't trust me.'

'I want to trust you, Anna, but you're being less than honest with me. You must admit that.'

'I haven't lied to you.'

'But you are keeping something from me.'

Anna looked over to the lake. 'There are things I can't tell you.'

'In that case,' Phil's voice was cold as he said, 'at the end of your three months' trial period, I suggest you take up your option to leave the company. And this time, let me assure you, there will be no way I will offer you your job back.'

'No, Phil, I . . . '

But Phil didn't look back as he strode off in the direction of Celeste's studio.

* ★ *

'Hello there,' Celeste greeted him as he entered the studio through the open double doors at the rear. 'Have you been for a walk through the grounds? Make the most of it. We may be turned out if this auction doesn't raise enough money to keep us afloat.'

'Celeste,' Phil said, 'mind if I make myself a coffee?'

'You know where it is.' Celeste wiped her paintbrush on a rag and placed it in one of her colourful holders. 'Sorry you missed Jenny, the physio. She wanted to have a quick word with you. Said she saw you talking to Anna and didn't like to disturb you. She also said it sounded like you two were having some sort of row.'

Phil emerged from the kitchen clutching a mug of coffee. 'Can I talk to you off the record, Celeste?'

'My, this sounds serious.' She wheeled her chair over to the coffee table. 'What's up?'

'It's Anna.'

Celeste's smile slipped. 'What about her?'

'You've known her a long time, haven't you?'

'Yes. A long time.'

'Exactly how well do you know her?'

Celeste hesitated. 'That's a difficult question to answer.'

'Would you say she was capable of cheating on me?' Phil asked.

Celeste's hand froze over a magazine she had been about to straighten. 'You're having an affair with Anna?'

'That's not what I mean.'

'Then I think you'd better explain yourself, Phil.'

'Anna wouldn't look twice at the likes of me. She's a Villiers, born and bred.'

'Don't talk like that.' Celeste's voice

was harsher than he had ever known it.

'I'm sorry,' he apologised, 'that was a stupid remark.'

'And an old-fashioned one. Anna may have been born into a privileged family, but she certainly wasn't over-indulged, and in answer to your question, Anna Villiers is not capable of cheating on anyone, professionally or otherwise.'

Celeste paused, then asked, 'Are you in love with her?'

'No, I'm not.'

'Well you ought to be. You are absolutely right for each other. You've got the brains when you're not being silly about a class difference that doesn't exist, and Anna's got brains and beauty. You would be a great team.'

'She's in the pay of Archie Wainwright,' Phil said.

'That's nonsense!' Celeste exploded.

'There's a picture of her in the Gazette with Hugh.'

'There are always pictures of her in the Gazette. In the past the Villiers were a very influential family in Ashton Vale.'

'She's young and bright. It's natural she's going to attract attention.'

'But let me assure you, Anna would rather be unemployed than work for Archie Wainwright.'

'She was pictured at a special black tie do Archie Wainwright had arranged for influential people he wanted to interest in this new planning project of his.'

'Just as well Anna was there, then. She's astute enough to sound out the opposition.'

'I would have agreed with you on that, except that she told me she hadn't seen Hugh in ages.'

'Did she indeed?' Celeste's lovely almond-shaped eyes narrowed.

'And I bumped into her outside Andy's office just now and she wouldn't tell me what she was doing here. She was supposed to be working from home, but she obviously wasn't.'

'She was here,' Celeste said.

'I know, I told you, I bumped into

her outside Andy's office.'

'No, I mean she was here, with me.'

'Anna was with you?' Phil frowned.

'Didn't I just say that? She was here all night, actually. There's a little camp bed we keep in the corner for when she sleeps over.'

Phil looked confused. 'I'm sorry? She sleeps over?'

'Why should she do that?'

'She often does. You see, sometimes I ring her father in the night if I can't sleep. He doesn't always sleep so well, either, so we chat about this and that.'

'That still doesn't explain what Anna was doing here all night.'

'I'd forgotten George was doing an overnight shift at the supermarket last night. I was having difficulty sleeping, so I rang Mallards. Anna answered the call. She came down here right away. I'm sorry. If she's in trouble, it's my fault.'

'Does she often spend the night here?'

'Yes, she does. I'm selfish, you see. I

love her company. I try not to be too demanding, but sometimes I can't help it. It's lovely having her all to myself. We chat, watch late night movies, things like that. Last night we did a bit of painting.'

Phil shook his head. 'I'd like to say I understand, but I don't.'

'I can't spend the night at Mallards, it's not designed for a wheelchair. That's why I had this little bed rigged up for Anna.' Celeste hesitated. 'George stays over as well, occasionally, when it's convenient.'

'Celeste, I don't think this is any of my business.' Phil was beginning to feel uncomfortable.

'Your private arrangements are none of my affair.'

'Look, I'm going to tell you something now, but before I do, you must promise me you won't let Anna know that you know, unless you really have to. Having sworn her to secrecy, I shouldn't be breaking her trust.'

'I'm not sure I understand.'

'I always wanted to make my own way as an artist, that's why I paint under my maiden name — Celeste Eden. I didn't want people thinking I'd traded on my married name.'

Celeste glanced down at her wedding ring. 'My married name is Villiers. George Villiers is my husband. Anna is my daughter.'

Phil Learns More Secrets

Stunned, Phil could only sit and look at Celeste in amazement. 'Anna is your daughter?'

'You noticed the resemblance the first time we met. Don't you remember?'

Phil looked hard at Celeste. The likeness was there. He could see that now. Celeste's eyes were of a greener hue than Anna's and her hair was raven. Anna's hair was soft with auburn tints, but she and her mother possessed the same pale skin, the same fine cheekbones and the same mannerisms. Anna tilted her head at a certain angle when she was challenging him and Celeste was looking at him in exactly the same way now.

'I assumed her mother had died when she was a child,' Phil said.

Celeste nodded. 'I thought you

might. I've lived here since Anna *was* a child and, despite my disability, I have tried to play as full a role in her life as possible.

'Her grandparents helped looked after her, but when they died, things became more difficult and the situation changed. Anna was sent away to boarding school and that's when things began to go downhill. George was working long hours trying to keep the family business afloat. He couldn't leave Anna alone in that big old house during the school holidays, so she began to spend time here.

'We had missed out on so much when she was younger, it was lovely to rediscover each other again as mother and daughter, and have time together, just the two of us. Then my painting took off and Anna went away to university.

'When she came back, we continued the tradition of spending our nights together whenever we could. I tell her about my life and she tells me about hers. I'm so proud of what she has achieved.'

'Then why don't you want people to know you're Anna's mother?' Phil said.

'Some do. Jenny knows and Andy, of course, and the Wainwrights. We don't make a secret of it, but we don't publicise it, either.'

'I still don't see why.'

'It is silly,' Celeste acknowledged, 'but you know what they say about old wounds having deep scars. When I first met George, his parents didn't approve of me. I was this wild Irish girl who had had the temerity to steal their son. They were the Villiers, the crème de la crème of the county. They could trace their family tree back to William the Conqueror.'

Phil raised his eyebrows in amused disbelief, conscious of an immense feeling of relief now he knew the real reason for Anna's being at Ash Park.

'Well, perhaps that is a bit of an exaggeration,' Celeste agreed, smiling, 'but they were rich and privileged, whereas my folk were of potato farming stock.

'To cut a long story short, George and I fell in love. We knew his parents would never agree to us getting married, so we eloped. We ran off to Italy before they could catch up with us.'

Celeste's fingers strayed to the painting on her easel. 'We went to the Villa St Helena.

'It was the most beautiful time of my life,' she said softly.

Phil's eyes strayed to her canvas. Celeste had painted it from the heart, and it showed.

'What happened after that?' he asked gently.

'We came back and made things up with his parents. Then, when I was expecting Anna, George joined the family firm, but his heart wasn't in it. He never was a businessman. I think he had aspirations to be a painter as well, but after my accident, our life changed again.'

Celeste went on, 'I fell off my horse

trying to jump a hedge. Anna wasn't much more than a baby at the time. I don't need to go into details. George's parents were truly marvellous and we actually grew very close when we no longer shared the family house together. Mallards is a very old property, as you know, and not suitable for wheelchairs. I couldn't live there anymore. A place became available at Ash Park, so I moved in here and began painting in earnest.'

'I used my maiden name because I didn't want to trade on my husband's family connections. I think George's father secretly approved of my independence. He was as proud as punch the first time I sold a painting, and we developed a sort of mutual respect after that.' Celeste clasped her hands together. 'So there you have it.'

As Phil looked at the beautiful woman in front of him, he could understand why George had fallen so in love with her he had defied his family. And hers was a beauty that would never fade.

'Thank you for telling me,' he said quietly.

'There was no intention to mislead you, Phil, and I did actually wonder if you already knew. I mean, you must have done a thorough check on my husband?'

'I ran a company's check, but I had no wish to pry into areas of your husband's private life.'

'No, I suppose you wouldn't.'

'I thought, when Anna mentioned a conflict of interest, she meant with the Wainwrights,' Phil said.

'She meant our relationship . . . hers and mine. We've always kept the Villiers Estates business separate from my painting.'

'Does that present us with another problem?' Phil asked.

'I don't understand.'

'The Open Day auction and your painting. There is a connection. You're painting the picture, and Anderson Villiers are doing the sponsoring.'

'I hadn't thought of that,' Celeste

admitted. 'Does it matter?'

'I don't mind if you don't mind, but I don't want to tread on any more toes.' He gave a rueful smile. 'I seem to be good at doing that lately.'

'It's not all you. The Villiers can be a twitchy lot, too.'

'Poor Anna,' Celeste sighed, 'none of this is her fault. Oh, but,' Celeste began searching through her handbag, 'I nearly forgot, the reason I telephoned you in the first place. Have you heard of a Damian Chancellor?'

'I've read about him. He's an agent. Used to be a financial wizard but his first love was the arts and one day he decided to change careers. He's been very successful, I believe.'

'He is. And he's seen my work and wants to represent me,' Celeste said. 'Read all about it.'

Phil took the letter Celeste handed to him and scanned it.

'Do you think I should see him?' she asked.

'Well, it can't do any harm to hear

what he has to say.'

'Can I come to you for help if I need it? If he offers a contract, something like that?'

'I'd be pleased to help.' Phil smiled at her with genuine affection. 'And thank you for telling me about Anna.'

'You're going to have to apologise to her again, you know,' Celeste pointed out.

'I seem to spend half my life doing that.'

'You know, Hugh Wainwright isn't the man for Anna . . . oh, come in, Jenny,' Celeste broke off what she was saying and waved at the physiotherapist who was hovering outside the swing doors.

'I'm not interrupting anything, am I?'

'No, I was just about to leave.' Phil picked up his jacket.

'It's you I want to talk to, actually, Mr Anderson.'

'If it's private, I can always take myself off,' Celeste volunteered. 'I usually take a turn round the gardens this time of day.'

But before Jenny could reply, the swing doors opened again.

'Celeste.' George Villiers bustled in with a huge box of Belgian chocolates. 'Thought these might cheer everyone up. I'll leave them on the table, shall I?' His eyes narrowed in concern. 'You're looking tired.'

'I didn't sleep too well last night. Don't be cross with me, George. Anna spent the night here.'

George cast an anxious look at Phil.

'It's all right, my dear. I've told Phil everything.'

A look of relief crossed George's face. 'I'm so pleased. I'm no good at secrets. The trouble is, my wife is so stubborn.'

He looked at Phil. 'Always wanted to do her own thing. The funny thing is, she's the most successful member of the family now.'

He turned back to Celeste. 'But you shouldn't have worried Anna, Celeste, she works such long hours and she needs her sleep. I've told you, I'll always come out for you.'

'I'm sorry, darling, I forgot you were working the night shift. When Anna answered the telephone I couldn't hang up on her. It was late and she might have thought it was a funny phone call. I had to speak to her.'

'And of course she rushed over here to be with you.'

'Yes. I tried to stop her, but she wouldn't hear of it. We watched television, then we talked into the small hours and then we overslept. My alarm didn't go off. I think I forgot to set it. Then Phil bumped into Anna outside Andy's office, so I had to tell him about us.'

Celeste put out a hand to George. 'Am I forgiven?'

George stroked her hand. 'Of course you are.'

It was a simple loving gesture, but it left Phil with the feeling he was intruding on a private moment. He coughed lightly. 'Anna and I had words,

I'm afraid. I'd jumped to all sorts of conclusions . . . '

'You haven't dismissed her again?' George demanded.

'No,' Phil said, 'we agreed on a three months' probation period. But after that,' he shrugged, 'we may be going our separate ways.'

Celeste picked up her jacket. 'Three months is an age. Things will sort themselves out, you'll see. George, Jenny needs to have a private word with Phil. Will you take me for a walk?'

George fussed round his wife, helping her with her jacket and chiding her for overworking.

*　*　*

Jenny closed the doors behind them, a smile lighting up her face. 'Lovely to see them together, isn't it? And I'm so glad you know about Anna now. She really is a wonderful girl.'

'So everyone keeps telling me..'

'Then you should try listening to

161

them.' Jenny held up her hands. 'Don't worry. I'm not going to lecture you. I actually need to talk to you about Hillcrest Farm.'

'Hillcrest Farm? What about it?'

'It's difficult to know where to begin.' Jenny smiled shakily, twisting her hands together. 'Have you heard about the latest development regarding Hillcrest Farm?'

Phil's brow cleared. 'Are you the Ash Park connection to Hillcrest Farm? George Villiers mentioned something about it the other day, only he wasn't sure exactly who it was.'

Jenny took a deep breath. 'Yes. My father's been living abroad for years. Samuel Tindall is his brother.'

'So it's your father who owns the ransom strip?'

'What's a ransom strip?' Jenny wanted to know.

'What it says, really. It's prime piece of land. If developers are after the rest of the property, the owner of the ransom strip can virtually name his price.'

Jenny nodded. 'I thought it would be something like that. My father was approached by Archie Wainwright and because he had been out of the country, he didn't know anything about the proposed new development. Archie Wainwright discussed terms with my father and drew up a contract. I'm a widow and I've got two young daughters and he wanted to give us the money to help my girls through school, that sort of thing.'

'I see. I had hoped to buy up the ransom strip myself, but it looks like Archie Wainwright's beaten me to it.'

'No. He hasn't.'

'I thought you said he had offered your father a good price?'

'He did, but my father didn't sign the contract. When I explained the position to him, he went back to his solicitor and had the land made over to me. I can show you the documentation if you'd like.'

'You own the ransom strip?'

'As of yesterday,' Jenny beamed at

Phil. 'And I've decided I'm going to sell it and I'd like you to handle the sale for me.'

'Don't do anything in a hurry, Jenny,' Phil cautioned. 'The price could rocket.'

'I'm not interested in making a fortune. I want just enough to see my daughters through college.'

'So, will you help me?'

Phil's head was reeling at this latest piece of news, but his professionalism took over as he answered, 'Of course. I can make an appointment with a financial adviser for you. One thing, though . . . '

'Yes?'

'Have you told anyone else about this?'

'Not yet.'

'Then I suggest you keep the information to yourself.'

'Right,' Jenny agreed. 'We don't want Archie Wainwright finding out about it, do we? Thank you, Phil.'

'My pleasure.'

And it was as Phil was driving away that Jenny remembered she had forgotten to tell him about Valerie Masters having lunch with Hugh Wainwright in the Anchor Hotel.

Valerie Has A Lot To Tell Anna

Valerie was placing a vase of orange chrysanthemums on her desk when Anna arrived for her work the next morning. 'Hope you don't mind,' Valerie said. 'Only I let myself in.'

'I didn't know you had a set of keys,' Anna frowned.

'Phil loaned me his set last night. He asked me to open up and he also asked me to tell you he wouldn't be in until later this afternoon. He's seeing a financial consultant.'

'You saw Phil last night?'

'Oh, yes, we went out for a meal.' Valerie switched on her computer then said, 'I'm not treading on your toes or anything, am I?'

'I've told you before, there's nothing between myself and Phil,' Anna said sharply.

'Yes, of course,' Valerie replied. 'You'd better have his set of keys back, hadn't you?' she smiled. 'I wouldn't want to lose them and I'm a bit scatty when it comes to things like that.'

Anna immediately regretted the sharp tone of her voice. 'Sorry, I didn't mean to snap,' she said, 'my wretched car played up again and I hate being late in.'

'Um . . . did you go somewhere nice last night?' she couldn't help asking.

'Actually,' Valerie confided, 'we didn't go anywhere. We ordered a takeaway and took it back to my flat and chatted about old times. It was a lovely evening. I wish you'd been with us.'

Anna wasn't entirely convinced Valerie was telling the truth on that one, but she let it go.

'I was working on those lost files and I managed to retrieve them,' she said, changing the subject.

'That is good news.' Valerie looked relieved.

'I still can't work out what happened

to the originals, Anna said.'

'Neither can Phil. He wanted to talk to you about them. I tried to get hold of you yesterday but you weren't answering your mobile. I left messages all over the place. Phil wasn't best pleased.'

'I'm sorry,' Anna apologised, not seeing the need to tell Valerie where she was. 'Now, was there anything urgent?'

'Not really.' Valerie smiled brightly. 'Phil was keen to trace those files, too, but as you've dealt with it, it would appear the problem's solved.'

'And there was nothing else?'

'Only an update on the plans for the Ash Park Open Day. Are you helping out on that one?'

'Not officially. I'm behind the scenes in the art room.'

'Lucky you. Celeste Eden is very 'in' at the moment, isn't she?'

'Yes, she is.' Anna did not look at Valerie. She didn't find it easy talking about her mother. And she'd had a rushed call from Celeste over breakfast.

'Did I get you into terrible trouble

yesterday, darling?' Celeste had gushed down the line, 'With Phil?'

Anna had been hopping round the kitchen, munching toast and looking for her shoes.

'Oh, but that's not why I rang,' Celeste didn't wait for Anna to reply. 'I had to ring you at this hideously early hour because I had to let you know.'

'Know what?' Anna gulped down some coffee and shrugged on her jacket.

'The first Saturday in June is the official date for the Open Day, so no more girly chats into the small hours for us. I'll be working my socks off.'

She rang off, leaving Anna feeling relieved. Celeste enjoyed her 'artist's hours' as she called them, but they played havoc with Anna's body clock.

Unlike her mother, Anna liked her full eight hours sleep every night — when she could get them.

'That was Mrs Tindall on the phone,' Valerie called over. 'She wants to know if Phil's taken any action on the ransom strip.'

'He hasn't yet,' Anna replied, 'or were there any developments yesterday that I don't know about?'

'Only the one about Jenny Barrow being the owner.'

'Sorry?' Anna looked up, the letter she was reading dropping from her fingers. 'What did you say?'

'Nothing.' Valerie tried to laugh it off. 'I shouldn't have said anything. Forget it.'

'Are you talking about Jenny, the physio at Ash Park?'

'Well, yes,' Valerie admitted. 'It turns out her father is Mr Tindall's brother. She's inherited the piece of land there's all the fuss about.'

'Who told you this?'

There was no mistaking the look of guilt that flashed across Valerie's face. 'Phil . . . ' she began.

'Phil wouldn't have discussed anything so confidential with you.' Anna paused before adding. 'No matter how close your relationship is.'

'He must have let it slip.'

'That's nonsense, Valerie, and you know it. Phil would discuss it with me first.'

'Well you weren't here yesterday for him to discuss it with, were you? Coffee?' And Valerie stood up and left the office.

Anna listened to her bustling around in the kitchenette. As soon as she heard the switch on the kettle, she strolled over to Valerie's desk. It was strewn with telephone call details and numbers. She picked up a slip of paper. On it was scrawled a number she recognised, one she had dialled several times herself.

She waited until Valerie came back in with the coffee tray.

'I didn't know you knew Hugh Wainwright,' she said casually.

Valerie slopped some coffee on Anna's desk. 'Hugh Wainwright?'

'This is his number, isn't it?'

'That's how you found out about Jenny, isn't it? It wasn't Phil. Hugh Wainwright told you.'

'It was Phil, I'm sure,' Valerie insisted. 'He must have told me last night. We had supper together. Remember?'

'It was Hugh Wainwright who told you, wasn't it?' Anna repeated.

'I don't know. I suppose it might have been. I really can't remember.'

'Exactly how long have you known Hugh Wainwright?'

'If you must know, he was a friend of my ex-husband's. He got in touch with me after he heard about my marriage break-up.'

'Why are you glaring at me, Anna? There's nothing wrong with that, is there?'

'Nothing at all, but I think you might have mentioned your connection with him.'

'The same way you mentioned attending Archie Wainwright's fund raiser?'

'That was different.'

'How different?'

'At least I haven't got my photo in

172

the Gazette holding hands with Hugh.'

'Yet you're accusing me of all sorts of things simply because I've got a note of his mobile number.'

Anna had to admit Valerie had a point. Was she over-reacting because she didn't trust Valerie Masters?

Was her mistrust based on the fact that Valerie was an old friend of Phil Anderson's?

An old friend who enjoyed intimate suppers with him.

If only she could tell Phil the truth, the real reason for her visit to Ash Park House, it would clear the atmosphere between them, but both her parents had agreed it would be better for them not to mention their connection with the therapy centre.

Anna hadn't quite followed her mother's reasoning, but she knew of Celeste's determination to keep her artistic work separate from the Villiers' business.

And as such she had to respect her mother's wishes.

Valerie sat down at her desk. 'Actually,' she said, 'Archie Wainwright has offered me a position working for him. I was going to give Hugh a call about it this evening.'

Anna looked up but didn't trust herself to say anything. 'The money's very good,' Valerie added, 'and this contract is only temporary, isn't it?'

'Are you giving in your notice?' Anna said.

'I have decided to accept Archie's offer, yes. Of course, I'll work my notice,'

'I see. Is there anything else you'd like to tell me?'

'Only that Hugh and I saw Jenny Barrow having lunch at The Anchor Hotel with a man. Hugh made some enquiries and found out it was her father and that his name was Jack Tindall. The rest was easy to work out.'

'And the lost files?' Anna demanded. 'You know what happened to them, don't you?'

Valerie's face was now very red. 'When we couldn't get hold of you yesterday, I sort of insinuated that you, well, might have been involved in losing them. But I don't think Phil believed me,' she added lamely.

'You did what?' Anna exploded.

'I know you didn't do anything with them, Anna. It was my fault. Technology has moved on since my day and,' Valerie paused. 'I pressed the wrong button. I deleted them. Then I panicked. I couldn't get them back. I've been so worried.'

'So you told Phil it was my fault?' Anna was outraged.

'I'm sorry. I was desperate. If Phil had known it was me, I would have been out on my ear, and I've got bills to pay. Not that it matters now, of course, since I've been offered the job with Archie Wainright.'

'Well it matters to me! I've got bills to pay, too. I can't afford to have my car serviced. That's why it keeps letting me down.'

'Yes, but you won't be thrown out of Mallards, will you?' Valerie retaliated with the hint of a sneer.

Anna drank some coffee to calm herself down.

'I feel bad about what I've done, Anna, but I promise I haven't passed on any confidential information to the Wainwrights. It was an unfortunate mistake. I am sorry,' Valerie said,

'Well,' Anna conceded, 'at least you've owned up to what you've done and, as you're now leaving us, there's no chance of you doing it again.'

'I will put things right with Phil, I promise. Actually, working for Hugh will be more my sort of thing. He mentioned public relations work, hostessing social events, that kind of thing. I'm not very good at paperwork and Phil's a very demanding boss.'

'If you really want to take up Hugh's offer, then I can't stop you. But perhaps you'd stay until the end of next week? I'll try and sort something out by then.'

'Er — actually — there is something

else I ought to tell you.' Valerie was still looking uncomfortable. 'Until last night I really was in two minds about accepting Hugh's offer.'

'What changed your mind?'

'I thought that maybe Phil and I could take up where we left off. It was only a very minor fling and it was years ago. In all I think we only had two dates. But I did like him a lot.'

'I don't think I want to hear any more, Valerie.'

'Last night, well the magic just wasn't there.' Valerie ploughed on, ignoring the interruption. 'I suppose the years lent a romantic gloss to what was really just a casual relationship.'

'You shouldn't be telling me all this.'

'Probably not, but I feel I owe you something to make up for blaming you for deleting those files. I really am sorry for all the trouble I've caused.'

Valerie looked so unhappy sitting at her desk, that Anna took pity on her. 'I didn't have much breakfast before I left home,' she said. 'Fancy a Danish while

I make some fresh coffee?'

'Good idea.' Valerie cheered up immediately and grabbed her purse. She turned before rushing out of the office.

'Would you come out for a meal with me one night, before I leave?' she asked. 'We could try that bistro down at The Marina? They say their lasagne's to die for. You can tell me all about Hugh. You grew up together, didn't you?'

'Yes, but really, there's not much to tell.'

'There's not much to tell about Phil, either. He's such a workaholic. I mean, there I was with the lights turned down low and the soft music playing, and he just wasn't interested.'

Anna tried to ignore the prickly sensation working its way up her spine. Valerie was the sort of girl who knew how to use her charms to full advantage. Yet they hadn't worked on Phil.

Celeste Is Nervous About The Open Day

Bunting flapped in the breeze. It was only ten in the morning, but the day was already warm and the temperature was set to rise. Volunteers sporting sunhats and T-shirts emblazoned with the Ash Park logo were liberally coating themselves with high factor sun protection.

'Going to be a good one, I think.' Andy Soames looked positively rakish in his striped blazer and white flannels.

'Get you,' Celeste whistled, as he strolled past her art display, clipboard in hand.

Andy raised his straw boater in acknowledgement of her greeting. 'Any sign of Damian Chancellor?' he asked. 'You don't want to miss him.'

'I know. But he's not here yet.'

'Well, tip me the wink the moment he appears.'

'Will do.' Celeste turned her attention back to her display. 'Steady,' she called out, as one of the porters nearly dropped her *Summer Days In Capri*.

'Sorry,' the porter apologised, hastily straightening the painting on its stand. 'Is that OK?'

'No. It's wonky. Better leave it to me.' Celeste wheeled herself across the grass. 'Go and see to the art school. Make sure they haven't made a total mess of the classroom.'

'No need to get your paintbrushes in a twist, Celeste.' Jack Tindall, Jenny's father, winked at her. 'I know you're nervous and all that, but this high-powered agent of yours can't fail to fall in love with you wearing that hat.'

'Do you think so?'

Like Andy, Celeste had dressed up. She was wearing a huge picture hat and a floaty frock she had borrowed from Jenny.

'I don't possess anything remotely dressy,' she had complained, when Andy had decided to adopt a twenties dress theme for the Open Day.

'I've got just the thing,' Jenny had suggested. 'It's only been worn once to a wedding and we're about the same size, so it should fit you perfectly.'

Celeste had to admit the salmon pink outfit went well with her dark hair, and the hat was so outrageous, it made everyone smile.

'If you're going to be the star of the day, Celeste,' Jenny did a few minor adjustments with hat pins, 'you've got to look the part. There,' she stepped back, 'that won't come off in a force ten gale.'

'Are you sure you don't want to wear it yourself?' Celeste had protested after inspecting her image in the mirror. She wasn't in the least bit vain but even she had to agree the outfit did something for her.

'I'm in uniform, worst luck. Someone's got to man the first-aid tent and I drew the short straw, so I'd better be off. Ask Anna to save me some strawberries and cream.'

'I'll see what I can do,' Celeste called after Jenny.

* * *

The Italian Lake held pride of place in the centre of the studio. Jack Tindall had done a good job of displaying it to best advantage, discreetly lit and standing on a curtained dais.

Celeste practised a few deep breaths to control the butterflies dancing in her stomach, then nearly jumped out of her skin as a hand landed on her shoulder.

'I can almost smell the lemons,' George whispered in her ear.

'Do you like it?' Celeste asked.

'I love it. You've so captured the essence of Santa Helena. And I love the donkey.' He pointed to the flower bedecked harness on the animal's panniers.

'I thought you would. It's my thank you to you for being so supportive. George?' Celeste squeezed his hand.

'What?'

'I'm nervous.'

'There's no need to be.'

'But we've so much riding on this. Supposing Damian doesn't like my work?'

'He will.'

'I may have pinned my hopes too high.'

'The Gazette has sent its star reporter to interview you. There's a photographer hovering outside itching to take your picture, and have you seen the length of the queue at the gate waiting to be let in?'

'You're a local celebrity, Celeste. Andy's blazer is almost bursting at the seams, he's so proud of you. Honestly, anyone would think this whole thing was his idea.'

'It was, wasn't it?'

'Correct me if I'm wrong, my darling, but the Santa Helena painting was most definitely your idea, and I don't remember there being three people on our honeymoon.'

'You know what I mean,' Celeste chided him.

'Believe me, Celeste, you have nothing to worry about. All your family and friends are here, and they are one hundred per cent behind you.'

'Talking of which, where is Anna?' Celeste said, looking around.

'In the refreshment tent doing a roaring trade in soft drinks and strawberries,' George told her.

'Is everything all right between her and Phil?' Celeste asked. 'I can't help worrying about her.'

'Anna can look after herself. Now, are you sure you've got everything?'

'I think so.'

'Right then. I'll be off.'

'Where are you going?' There was a note of panic in Celeste's voice.

'You know I've got to work in the

supermarket until lunch-time.'

'Sorry,' Celeste apologised, 'I forgot.'

'The manager and most of the staff have promised to drop by some time during the day, so you'll have lots of support. Remember, we're all on your side.'

Celeste patted George's arm and looked up into his smiling face. 'It's a long while since I've seen you so happy,' she said.

'It's a long while since I've been so happy.'

'It's such a pity you've got to go into work. You should have asked for the day off.'

'I know, but some of the youngsters wanted to come and I thought it only fair to let them.'

'All the same, it's a shame you couldn't be here for the grand opening. Did I tell you I'm cutting the ribbon?'

'Once or twice.' A smile curved George's lips. 'I'll be here in time for the auction, I promise.' He gave Celeste a kiss. 'See you later.'

After George had gone, Celeste tried to busy herself in the studio, but it had already been polished to within an inch of its life by an army of cleaners. In the distance, she saw Anna struggling with a tea urn. She waved, but her daughter didn't see her.

A shadow flitted across Celeste's face. Despite George's assurances, her maternal instinct told her Anna wasn't happy. She suspected it was something to do with Phil Anderson, but Anna wouldn't be drawn. Ever since Celeste's talk with Phil, when she'd revealed she was Anna's mother, she had longed to tell her daughter that Phil knew of their relationship, but the moment was never right. There hadn't been any more sleepovers at Ash Park and only hurried phone calls between them.

Celeste stroked the soft silk of her outfit. Rumours were rife. Archie Wainwright had failed in his bid to buy the strip of land in the middle of Hillcrest Farm, and, if today was a success, his plans for Ash Park might fall through as well. Celeste didn't really understand any of what was going on, but Jenny seemed to know and had kept Celeste up to date.

'Ms Eden?' She looked up. 'Sorry, I didn't mean to startle you. I'm Damian Chancellor.'

Standing in the doorway of the studio was a middle-aged man, dressed rather inappropriately in a pin-striped suit and crisp white shirt and carrying a briefcase.

'Come in,' Celeste gulped. The fluttering feeling in her chest was back. 'I'm sorry you had to find your own way here. There was supposed to be a welcome committee to greet you.'

'One of the tent poles has collapsed,' Damian smiled. 'I think it was a case of greeting me or saving the strawberries, and the strawberries won the day.'

He had an open, friendly face and Celeste warmed to him immediately.

'I have to admit, Mr Chancellor . . . ' she began.

'Damian, please.'

'Very well, Damian, I've been reading up on you. You were a City whiz kid, weren't you?'

'For my sins. Yes.'

'May I know why you gave it all up?'

'I'd got to a certain age when I decided I wanted more out of life and if I didn't do something about it soon, I never would. Art was always my first love and I did go to Art College, but my father died and so I had to leave and get a proper job. There is a lot more I could tell you about my disreputable past.' He smiled again. 'But perhaps another time?'

'You didn't have to tell me as much as that, but thank you.' Celeste folded her hands in her lap in an attempt to stop them shaking. 'Well, this is it, the moment of truth. Would you like to look round on your own? I can make myself scarce if you would prefer.'

Damian had walked towards *The Italian Lake* while Celeste had been speaking. He didn't appear to have heard a word she'd said. He gazed at the painting in silence. Celeste held her breath and waited.

'This is breathtaking,' he said at last. He put out a hand as if to touch the picture and then withdrew it. 'Don't want to set the alarms off.'

'There aren't any,' Celeste said.

'There should be. Celeste Edens are changing hands at phenomenal prices. And you've got a room full of them with no alarms.' He looked shocked.

'I seriously doubt anyone would try to take off with one,' Celeste smiled. 'And if they tried, there's a regiment of helpers to get past, and they might just notice a canvas tucked under someone's arm.'

'This is the piece intended for the auction?' Damian asked.

'Yes. We were hoping you would do the honours Mr, er, Damian.'

'My pleasure, Celeste. And as for that

contract,' he patted his briefcase, 'shall we say it's in the bag?'

* * *

'There you are Mr Chancellor.' A very red in the face Andy hurried towards them. 'I'm so sorry I missed you.'

'That's quite alright. Celeste and I have already introduced ourselves.' Damian shook hands with Andy.

'Damian has agreed to be our host for the auction,' Celeste said.

'Wonderful news,' Andy beamed. 'I have a feeling the day is going to a rip-roaring success! Let me introduce you to the Board of Trustees.'

'May I steal him away, Celeste?'

The look Damian threw over his shoulder told Celeste he would far rather stay where he was.

* * *

Celeste wheeled herself outside and over towards the tea tent, bursting to tell Anna her good news. She also wanted to have a word with Phil Anderson, but so far this morning she hadn't seen him.

'Anna, darling,' she called over, 'have you seen Phil?'

'He was in a meeting with Andy, I think.' A shuttered look came over Anna's face. 'Would you like a drink?'

'Not right now.'

Crowds were already pouring through the entrance gates, and, mindful of Damian's warning about security protection, Celeste headed back across the lawn towards her studio. Telling Anna about Damian would have to wait.

'Jack,' she called out to Jenny's father, 'can you get one of the porters to keep an eye on the paintings? Make sure no-one touches anything? And can you organise a viewing rota? We don't want too many people in the studio at the one time.'

'Leave it to me, Celeste.'

'There she is,' Celeste heard someone

say, as cameras were pointed in her direction.

She turned her head away. Having her photo taken was one of her least favourite occupations.

'You're supposed to look that way.' Jenny pointed towards the battery of lenses. 'They're from the press and I didn't lend you that outfit for you to hide yourself away.'

'Sorry,' Celeste apologised. 'I'm not used to all this attention.'

'Phil!' she saw his tall figure in the background and called out his name in relief. 'Come and rescue me.'

'Give Ms Eden some room,' Phil said, as he took charge of Celeste's wheelchair. 'Thank you.'

'Now I've got news for you, Celeste,' he told her as he pushed her towards the studio.

'Me first,' Celeste interrupted. 'Damian's agreed to take me on.'

'I know.'

'You know?' Celeste could not disguise her disappointment that her surprise was ruined.

'I've been talking to him, and guess what?' Phil said.

'He's going to bid millions for *The Italian Lake*?'

'Nearly. We've had an anonymous donation to set up a trust fund for struggling artists on the understanding that they reside at the centre! Andy is going to make a big announcement at the auction. Damian has agreed to chair the project. So unless there are any last minute hiccups, and with Damian Chancellor on our side, it looks very much as though Ash Park House has been saved.'

There Is Fantastic News

The studio, renamed the auction room in honour of the occasion, was buzzing with excited visitors.

Anna had been rushed off her feet in the refreshment tent, serving cups of tea and cakes to an army of visitors. Custom only began easing off when Andy rang a bell and announced that the auction was about to begin. Anna poured herself a quick glass of water before following the crowds making their way across the lawn towards the studio.

Ash Park hadn't seen so much excitement in years and every available space was taken. Celeste had offered to save her a place in the front row, but Anna had declined. It was Celeste's day and she decided the front row would be best kept for visiting dignitaries.

Anna spotted an empty place behind

a pillar and managed to nab it. It wasn't until she'd squashed into the seat that she realised the one next to her was occupied by Phil Anderson. The pillar had obscured his tall figure. She looked at him in dismay.

Ever since their confrontation over two weeks ago, and without Valerie's presence in the office to defuse the tension, relations between them had been strained.

'Why can't we keep a receptionist?' Phil had demanded, after Valerie had given in her notice.

'You lost the first one,' Anna had pointed out, 'and,' she added, 'employing Valerie on a temporary basis was your idea.'

'This will mean sharing her duties again.' Phil hesitated. 'Are you sure you don't mind? It will mean a lot of extra work.'

The tone of his voice softened, causing Anna to frown. If she didn't know better, she would have suspected him of being concerned for her.

'I've done it before,' had been her reply.

★　★　★

'You're wearing cricket whites.' Her voice was full of surprise as Phil turned to look at her.

'And you look great as a flapper.'

Anna wished his smile wasn't quite so welcoming. It made it difficult for her to remember that he didn't trust her.

'I couldn't think what to wear,' Anna confessed, looking down at her grandmother's striped silk dress. 'I went through a trunk in the attic and found this.

'But you look,' Anna only just managed not to say, 'fantastic'. 'You look fit,' she said instead.

'I don't feel it. I've moved around more chairs and tables today than I have for many a day.'

'You should try manning a tea urn.'

He carried on smiling into her eyes

and Anna wanted to turn away, but found she couldn't.

'I need to speak to you,' Phil said urgently. 'Later?'

* * *

Before Anna could reply, there was a buzz in the audience as Andy mounted the podium to start the proceedings.

'Ladies and gentlemen,' he announced, 'it is my very great pleasure to welcome you to the Ash Park Open Day. We are today honoured to have as our guest, the very famous Damian Chancellor.

'Damian has very kindly agreed to run our auction of paintings by our artist in residence, Celeste Eden, who of course needs no introduction.'

All eyes went to Celeste as the applause reached ear-deafening level. 'Now, I won't hold the proceedings up any longer, so it's over to you, Damian.'

* * *

Anna's eyes widened as painting after painting was knocked down at prices way beyond Celeste's estimates.

'I had no idea people spent such money on art,' she whispered to Phil as *Summer Days In Capri* was knocked down for a four-figure sum.

'Your — I mean, Celeste, is a voice of her generation,' Phil whispered back.

'What's that supposed to mean?' Anna demanded.

'Haven't a clue,' Phil grinned back at her, 'but I heard one of that lot say it and thought it was worth repeating.'

He nodded towards a small group of men busily ticking off the lots in their catalogues.

*　*　*

And now,' Damian said, as a hush descended on the room as *The Italian Lake* was taken off its stand and brought to the centre of the stage, 'the reason why we are all here today. Ladies and gentlemen, may I present to you

The Italian Lake, a truly remarkable piece of work executed by Celeste Eden at the special request of the trustees of Ash Park House.

'All money raised for its sale will go to the Foundation, which as some of you may already know, has today also received an anonymous donation. The bequest is to be used to aid the careers of young artists,' the rest of Damian's announcement was drowned by the roars of approval and applause that broke out in the audience.

'Did you know about this?' Anna asked Phil.

'I heard the final details this afternoon. I wanted to tell you myself, but Damian's beaten me to it. Great news, isn't it?'

'It's wonderful.'

'Look,' Phil pointed across the room, 'isn't that Archie Wainwright?'

'He's not looking too happy, is he?' Anna grinned.

'I'm not surprised. It's the end of his deal. He's lost Ash Park and Hillcrest Farm.'

A surge of elation swept through Anna. 'We did it!' she said. 'We've beaten him! We've won. Ash Park is saved.'

In an unthinking gesture of spontaneity, she hugged Phil's arm. It was strong under her touch and she felt Phil take her hand. Embarrassed, she pulled it back.

Damian banged his gavel in an effort to silence the audience. Whoops of joy from Celeste's art students were slow to die down, but eventually the studio returned to some semblance of normality.

'Ladies and gentlemen,' Damian announced, 'I would now like to open the bidding for The Italian Lake.'

Anna listened in amazement as the bidding grew fast and furious. Eventually it was whittled down to two determined bidders, neither of whom Anna could see, but heads were turning swiftly from left to right as the auction went on.

'What about your reserve?' Anna said

anxiously to Phil. 'You can't possibly match these prices.'

'Doesn't look like I'll need to. I think there's going to be enough money to cover everything without my contribution.'

'Going once,' Damian hesitated, glancing at the second bidder, who shook his head, 'going twice. Sold.' He banged down his gavel for the final time. 'And that, ladies and gentlemen, concludes the auction.'

Anna saw a distinguished looking white-haired gentleman get out of his seat to shake Celeste's hand — the proud purchaser of *The Italian Lake*. She was pleased to see Celeste was also smiling. It wasn't unknown for her to go against purchasers of her paintings. There had been one or two uncomfortable incidents in the past when work had had to be withdrawn from sale and a diplomatic excuse made as to why it was no longer on the market. Thankfully, it didn't look like that was going to happen today.

'Isn't it absolutely fantastic?' Anna jumped as Jenny poked her head through the open window and somehow managed to reach across her and hug Phil. 'I'm so pleased. I've got to kiss you. Thank you.' Laughing, Phil steadied her as they embraced.

Anna had never seen Jenny so happy. Her face was wreathed in smiles. 'See you later,' she said to them both when she and Phil drew apart. 'I'd better get back to base camp. I'm doing a roaring trade in this heat. I've never had to deal with so many funny turns.'

Anna could sympathise with that one. She was beginning to feel uncomfortable herself in the cramped room.

But before she could get up to go, a voice said, 'You look very dashing, Phil,' and Valerie was standing in front of them in long yellow gloves and a yellow flapper dress. She kissed Phil on the cheek.

'Hello Anna.' Another voice joined in. 'Long time no see.'

'Hugh.' He looked very distinguished

in college cap and gown.

'That's a lovely outfit you're wearing,' he said. Anna smiled back reluctantly.

'Am I allowed to ask you out on another date?' he murmured in her ear, casting a look at Phil, who was still talking to Valerie, 'or am I off limits?'

'I don't know. Give me a call.'

She didn't care if Phil overheard them. Hugh was her oldest friend and, as it looked like their business differences had now been settled, she was free to date who she liked.

'You're on,' Hugh's response was more enthusiastic than Anna would have liked.

'On for what?' Valerie enquired.

'Just catching up on old times with Anna,' Hugh answered smoothly.

Valerie slipped a proprietorily arm through his. 'We mustn't waste any more of Phil and Anna's time. You promised me a drink, remember?'

★　★　★

Once Hugh and Valerie had gone, Anna whispered to Phil, 'How soon can we leave, do you think?'

'Things look like they're closing down and there's an army of helpers to clear up. You've done enough for one day. Why don't we make our goodbyes and slip away? And are you free for dinner this evening?'

The invitation took Anna by surprise. She glanced across to where her parents were deep in conversation with Damian Chancellor. A family get together had been suggested earlier in the week, but no more mention had been made of it and Celeste could be forgetful about dinner dates on occasions like this. Anna gestured across the room and received a casual wave in return from her mother.

'Dinner?' Phil was still looking at her. 'I — er, yes, dinner would be lovely.'

* * *

Phil guided her through the milling throngs of people towards the car park.

'Where's your car?'

'In the garage again. I had to cadge a lift off Jenny.'

'Then we'll use mine. Over here.'

In honour of the occasion, Phil's four track had been through the car wash, and it looked more respectable than usual.

'Didn't your father make allowance for you to have a company car?' Phil asked, as he turned the engine.

'We had several,' Anna admitted, 'but mine was the first to go. It made sense. Besides, an old aunt gave up driving at the same time and she passed her car on to me. Trouble was, the car was nearly as old as she was.'

'I had no idea,' Phil said.

'It's a lovely car, when it works, but lately it's been throwing hissy fits. Still, the mechanics are working on it all weekend. Actually, Phil,' Anna began, 'about . . . '

'Not now. Need to concentrate,' Phil said, not taking his eyes off the road. Revellers were slowly wending their way home, several on foot and most in jubilant mood.

By now the heat was leaving the day. Anna leaned back in her seat. She felt exhausted, but elated. Her problems were over. Ash Park House was safe from the property developers. She closed her eyes. She was too tired to think about her future. She was too tired to think about anything. Moments later she was asleep.

Phil Confesses His Feelings

'Wake up, sleepyhead.' Anna opened her eyes. Phil was leaning over her, smiling.

'Where are we?' She yawned and stretched and felt something constricting her arms. 'What's this?'

'My jumper. You looked a bit cold.'

Anna breathed in deeply. She could smell the scent of Phil's body on the wool. It was a heady experience.

'Did I fall asleep?' she asked, blinking up at him.

'You went out like a light,' Phil said. 'I almost hate to disturb you, but we've arrived.'

Anna scrambled out of the passenger seat. They were parked on the residents' private forecourt outside Phil's flat.

'I thought we were going out to dinner.'

'I need to freshen up first.' His face softened as he looked at her, 'and while you look as fresh as a daisy, your feather has definitely seen better days.'

Anna snatched her velvet headband off. Her head immediately felt cooler, but her face didn't. The expression in Phil's eyes was sending her temperature rocketing.

'I — er, yes, good idea. Um, which floor do you live on?' Anna knew she was wittering, but she was feeling unaccountably nervous. 'I always liked Nightingales.' She looked up at the ivy-clad Victorian building. It was an old house that had been split up into exclusive private apartments. Anna knew the house well. Many years ago, she had attended a children's birthday party here, but several years later, the family had moved abroad and after that, the house had been converted into flats. Anna's father had been involved in the renovation and sale of the first flats. It had been one of his last professional undertakings with Villiers.

* ★ ★

Phil's flat was on the second floor and the lounge had panoramic views over the extensively landscaped gardens.

'It's lovely up here.' Anna looked out onto the terrace to where huge tubs of purple hydrangeas spilled out over the old moss-covered stone. 'I'm glad they haven't cleaned up the stonework too much.'

'I agree.' Phil was standing by her side. 'These old properties don't need much structural work on them. Houses were soundly built in those days, but people like Archie Wainwright can't see that.'

Anna turned and nearly collided with Phil. She hadn't realised he was standing so close to her.

'Would you like a drink?' he asked.

'I'd love a cup of tea.'

'The bathroom's at the end of the corridor if you want to freshen up,' Phil said, 'I'll put the kettle on.'

Thankful to have a valid reason to

remove herself from his presence, Anna hurried out of the lounge and headed for the bathroom. It was large and open plan with mosaic tiles and clean, unfussy accessories. A huge old-fashioned tub with heavy brass taps stood in the middle of the room and Anna would have loved to indulge in a long hot soak, but when Phil had invited her to freshen up, she was sure he hadn't meant her to wallow in a bath of fragrant bubbles.

She went over to the hand basin and tried to repair the ravages of the day. Her silk ensemble didn't look too world weary, and a quick flick of water through her hair soon had her tangled curls resembling something like normality. She washed her face and hands with the plain unscented soap in the dish. It left her nose rather shiny, but Anna hadn't the energy to reapply her make up, besides which, her handbag with all her make-up was still in the lounge.

'You'll have to do,' she said, as she inspected her reflection.

Considering she had been on her feet since six that morning, she was surprised she was still standing. She stifled another yawn and hoped it wasn't going to be a late evening and that Phil hadn't make plans to go out to a smart restaurant. She might be in danger of falling asleep in the soup.

'There you are,' he greeted her, as she made her way back to the lounge. 'Slice of lemon? I've run out of milk.'

'Lovely.'

Phil was seated on the sofa and Anna hesitated before sitting down next to him.

'We should have got together socially before now.' Phil said, 'but there hasn't been time.'

Anna toyed with her teaspoon, uncertain what to say next. She watched Phil pour out his own tea and drink it down.

'I needed that,' he said.

The collar of his cricket shirt was undone and Anna found her eyes fixed on the well of his neck. His skin looked taut and suntanned.

'What's the matter?'

'Sorry,' it was her turn to apologise, 'been a busy day. Think I'm a bit brain dead.'

'Me too. Tell you what, why don't we send out for something to eat? That new Vietnamese place had a good write up in the Gazette. Want to try it?'

Anna nodded, not feeling in the least hungry, but thankful Phil hadn't suggested one of the smart new restaurants on the waterfront.

'Tell you what, you order something while I change out of this kit. Won't be long. The telephone is on the coffee table.'

Thankful to be alone again, Anna leafed through the directory and found the number of the takeaway place. She ordered their meal, then finished her tea and took the tray through to the kitchen.

The view from the kitchen window looked over what was the old tennis court. Anna remembered playing tennis there with her school friend before she and her family emigrated. In those days, she hadn't a care in the world. Her grandparents were still alive and she had been cocooned in a life of love and luxury. Yet, behind the scenes, her life was already beginning to fall apart.

★ ★ ★

Once back in the lounge, she heard a noise behind her. Phil had changed from his cricket whites into casual chinos and a sweatshirt.

'I'm not sure what I've ordered,' Anna confessed as he joined her, 'but they said it would take about twenty minutes.'

'Fine. Let's have some music.' Phil flicked on a table lamp and searched through his CDs.

The next moment the overture to Figaro flooded the room and Anna leaned back against the sofa cushions.

'I wonder who our mystery benefactor is,' she said, as Phil eased himself down next to her.

'Tell you what,' the gentle lighting softened the harsher planes of his face, making him look almost vulnerable. Anna's pulse quickened. This was a Phil she couldn't deal with. She was used to confrontation. That way it was easy to keep him at arm's length.

She didn't want a Phil who suffered the same human emotions as everyone else. With her own defences down, she didn't know if she was up to meeting such an onslaught on her senses.

'W . . . what?' she stuttered, trying and failing to sit upright.

'I suggest we don't talk about work or anything vaguely connected with it. Agreed?'.

'Yes. Fine.'

Anna wasn't sure if it was fine, but she would have agreed to anything just to stop Phil looking at her like he was doing.

'You start first,' she said, in an attempt to lighten the atmosphere. 'Tell me about your family.'

Phil hesitated. 'I was brought up in Bath, but you already knew that, didn't you?'

Anna settled back into the softness of the cushions. 'I think so.' She couldn't really remember, but she was anxious to keep the conversation on neutral territory. 'Were you born there?'

'No. I was born in Scotland.'

'And your parents were a vicar and his wife?'

'How do you know that?' Phil asked, looking surprised.

Anna bit her lip, remembering it was Celeste who had told her. 'Er, I think I must have read something somewhere.'

Phil let that pass.

'Have you got any brothers or sisters?' Anna asked.

'One sister. She's married with two children.'

'Would you like to be married?' The question was out before Anna realised she had asked it. 'Sorry, none of my business.'

The doorbell rang. 'That'll be the

takeaway,' Phil got to his feet, 'and in answer to your question, yes, when the right person comes along.'

★ ★ ★

Anna could only put her light-headedness down to hunger. All she'd had all day had been the snatched glass of water before the start of the auction. Her stomach rumbled as Phil came back with their meal.

'Whatever we've got, it smells good. You sort it out while I see what I've got to drink.'

Anna took out the foil containers and peeled back the covers. A fragrant smell of lemon and herbs and spices made her mouth water.

'No wine, I'm afraid.' Phil was back. 'I haven't had time to go shopping for weeks. There's this.' He produced a carton of fresh orange juice, and poured out two glasses.

They ate in silence for several minutes. The light had slowly drifted from the day and by the time they had finished their meal, there was only the gentle glow from the table lamp lighting the room.

Anxious to do something with her hands, Anna stacked the foil containers and put them into a carrier bag, all the while aware of Phil's eyes on her.

'Phil, I . . . ' Anna began, wondering if he could also sense the tension.

'Don't say anything.' His voice was thick, as if he didn't quite understand what was happening, either.

Anna closed her eyes. It had to be stopped. There was too much baggage between them for this to happen. She felt his arms go round her and stiffened.

'I can't.' She tried to draw away from him, but didn't quite manage to escape his embrace. Possibly because she didn't want to.

'I've tried to fight it, Anna, but it's no good. I've got to tell you how I feel about you,' Phil said. 'Everyone kept sticking up for you and I never heard anyone utter a bad word about you. First there was Sally telling me I was fool of the first order, then Jenny Barrow, Andy, Celeste, your father, joined in the general praise. I knew I couldn't fight it any longer when Valerie told me I was fool not to realise what was staring me in the face.'

'Don't,' Anna begged, 'don't go on. There are things about me you don't know.'

'There aren't, Anna. I know . . . '

Inside her handbag her mobile phone began to ring.

'Leave it,' Phil said.

'I have to answer it.' Anna drew away from him. 'It might be Ash Park.'

'Anna?' Celeste's voice came at her down the line. 'Darling, I'm so sorry I missed you. Why did you rush off like that after the auction? I have to see you. Can you get over here right away?'

Emotional Blackmail
From Hugh

'I have to go.' Anna told Phil. 'It's Celeste.' Phil looked at his watch. 'Now? It's late.'

'Celeste often works into the night — her artist's hours she calls them.'

'I'll drive you over then. Luckily we've only been drinking orange juice.'

'I can call a cab.' Anna's head was still reeling. Why did Celeste have to pick that moment to call? And what had Phil been about to tell her? She loved her mother and father so much, but between them they had complicated her life. If only she could tell Phil the truth about her relationship to Celeste . . . but a promise was a promise. Phil would never find out from Anna that Celeste Eden was her mother.

Phil was looking at her with an almost sad expression. 'Anna,' his voice was soft, 'if you really would prefer asking a stranger to drive you through the night back to Ash Park, then I won't object.' He paused as if searching for the right words. 'I realise I spoke out of turn just now. I'm sorry. It won't happen again.'

'No, it isn't that,' Anna interrupted quickly. 'There are . . . well, things I can't explain.'

Phil nodded with a tired smile. 'As you wish. Now, shall we go? Or would you really prefer to ring for a mini cab?'

Anna realised she was being foolish. Cabs on a Saturday night in Ashton Vale were difficult to get If she phoned for one she could be in for a long wait.

'I didn't mean to sound ungrateful,' she told Phil. 'A lift to Ash Park would be very welcome. Thank you.'

'Right then, let's go.'

★   ★   ★

Phil began looking round for his keys. He picked up the cricket sweater he had discarded earlier. 'You'd better borrow this. The night air can be quite cold.'

'Thank you,' Anna said with a smile, but Phil had already turned away for his jacket.

The magic of the moment was gone and Anna doubted it would ever return.

Phil had taken her words as rejection, but they weren't a rejection. She was beginning to realise she was falling in love with him. And it wasn't as if she had been drinking wine or was light-headed. Her mind was perfectly clear and it was telling her she was in love with Phil Anderson. But she could never tell him how she felt. Nor could she ever explain the reason for her actions in fending him off.

They barely spoke on the ride back to Ash Park. Anna snuggled inside Phil's sweater. Although the day had been warm and it wasn't yet completely dark, she shivered, whether as a reaction from her emotions or the cool night air, she wasn't sure. Had Phil been going to say his feelings for her ran deeper than that of professional colleagues? And what would she have done if he had?

Well, she would never know now, since Celeste's call had interrupted him.

Celeste. Why had she called? Anna hadn't been paying full attention to what she said, but there had been a lot of noise in the background. It didn't sound like an emergency and she was sure her father would have stayed with Celeste after the auction.

* * *

Phil drew off the road and down the lane that led to Ash Park House. Bunting still fluttered round the gates and a huge banner proclaiming the open day flapped at them.

'Here we are,' Phil said, as they drew up at the front entrance.

'Thank you.' Anna opened the passenger door, then turned back to Phil.

'Would you like to come in for a few moments? I'm sure Celeste would be pleased to see you. She hasn't really had a chance to thank you.'

A small hope flared inside Anna; maybe her mother could be persuaded to tell Phil of their relationship.

'It's been a long day,' Phil's voice was impassive. 'I think I'll get on home. I need a bath and my beauty sleep.'

It was a diplomatic turn down.

* * *

Anna could see the studio lights in the distance. It looked like Celeste was holding a party. She would have to attend. Everyone would be there — everyone except Phil.

'I'll, um, I'll see you in the office on Monday?' she said.

'Yes. No doubt. Have a good week-end.'

They were speaking like polite strangers.

Phil had already re-started the car as

223

Anna climbed out. She didn't stay to watch him drive away.

* * *

As she got closer to the studio, she could hear voices and laughter and music — all the sounds of a celebration.

'Darling,' Celeste was outside the door. 'There you are. I was worried about you. I was wondering where you were. I'm just getting a breath of air. Everyone seems to want to speak to me tonight. I'm so sorry I forgot our dinner date, but you disappeared before I could have a word with you and things were so hectic, I didn't have a chance to — what on earth are you wearing?' She peered at Anna through the twilight.

'Phil's cricket jumper. I went back to his flat.'

'Where is he?' Celeste asked eagerly. 'I haven't thanked him properly for all his help.'

'He couldn't stay.'

Celeste's eyes narrowed. 'I see. Is

something wrong between you?'

'No. Nothing.'

'Tell me to mind my own business, if you like, but a mother's intuition tells me there is.'

'No,' Anna said firmly, 'there's nothing wrong. And before you ask, there's nothing of a personal nature between Phil and me.'

Celeste put out a hand to Anna. 'That's a pity. I like Phil Anderson. He's a good man.'

'Can we not talk about him?' Anna said uneasily, aware that Celeste was more than astute when it came to this sort of thing.

'As you wish, darling.' Celeste shook her daughter's hand gently. 'Now come and join the party. Everyone is here. That gorgeous Mr Chancellor, Damian, I mean, has offered me a contract that will keep me in canvases for years to come.' Celeste laughed in delight. 'Oh, I feel so happy. Ash Park is no longer under threat. What a wonderful day.'

'I had no idea I knew so many people,' Celeste waved across the room to a group of people trying to attract her attention. 'Must go and mingle. Enjoy yourself, darling.'

Anna stood uncertainly on the threshold of the party. She blinked. The lights were bright in her eyes. She had never felt less like a party in her life.

'Hello. Been practising in the nets?' Hugh joked, as he appeared at her elbow.

'What? Oh, it's Phil's,' Anna explained, shrugging off his cricket jumper and draping it over the back of a chair. 'He lent it to me.'

Hugh raised his eyebrows. 'So the rumours are true?'

'What rumours?'

'About you and Phil. Valerie's been going round saying that the pair of you are an item.'

'She's got no right to do that!'

'You've got to admit it is a bit

suspicious when you attend a party draped in his cricket jumper. What are people going to think?'

'It's none of their business! And you can tell your gossiping friends that, when my three month contract is up, Phil and I will be parting company.'

Hugh widened his eyes in surprise. 'You're not staying on at Anderson Villiers?'

'We're . . . ' Anna searched for the right word, 'incompatible.'

Hugh squeezed Anna's hand. 'I'm so pleased to hear it. So does this mean you're available?'

'I've told you before, Hugh, I can't work for your father. His ideas and mine are different. Besides, hasn't he offered the job to Valerie?'

'I wasn't talking about the job, I was talking about you and me.'

'There is no you and I, Hugh. You know that. And there's no point in going over old ground.'

Anna didn't want to hurt Hugh's feelings and tried to soften the blow by suggesting, 'so let's have a drink? As friends?'

'Whatever you say.'

Hugh did not return her smile.

★   ★   ★

'Wonderful news, isn't it?' Jenny bumped into them as they made their way to the drinks table. 'I can't believe we pulled it off. Where's Phil?' She looked over Anna's shoulder. 'He's not here,' Anna said.

Jenny frowned. 'Didn't I see you drive up with him?'

Anna brushed Jenny's question aside, aware that Hugh was looking at her. 'He gave me a lift, that's all. He couldn't stay for the party.'

'What a shame. If it hadn't been for him, none of this would have come about.'

'What do you mean?' Anna said.

Jenny made a face. 'Sorry. I think I've said too much. Better go and do some networking before I put my foot in it any more. Catch up with you later.'

'What was all that about, do you think?' Anna asked Hugh as he poured out two glasses of wine.

'No idea,' Hugh admitted. 'Phil did put in a lot of work arranging the auction so I suppose she could be referring to that, but everyone worked hard, your mother in particular. And I must say, success suits her.'

Anna looked round the studio. The podium had been cleared to make room for the party. There was no sign of *The Italian Lake*, but the other paintings were still hanging on the walls, most of them sporting little red 'sold' dots. They reflected her mother's life, her work, and Anna could not have been happier for her. Her father too, laughing and chatting by her side, seemed more content these days now he was no longer weighed down by the responsibility of Anderson Villiers.

'Yes,' Hugh was saying, 'your mother will really miss not being a part of all this.'

Anna frowned. Had she missed something Hugh had said? 'Sorry? What was that?'

'The studio,' Hugh swept out a hand indicating the paintings. 'Now she's got an agent, she'll need bigger and better facilities.'

'But she's not moving.'

'She may have no choice.'

'I don't understand what you're saying, Hugh. There isn't a problem with Ash Park, is there? That's what this party is all about, isn't it? Or have you heard something?'

'Not officially, no.'

'But?' Anna prompted.

'If this anonymous donor, whoever he is, should remove his funding, there could be a problem.'

'But he won't.'

'We don't know that.'

'What would be the point of making the offer in the first place?'

'There might be certain conditions attached to it.'

'Such as?'

'A thirty-day cooling off period? That sort of thing.'

Anna shook her head. 'No-one mentioned anything about any conditions.'

'They wouldn't make it public, but it would make good business sense. There's always a get-out clause in these contracts, in case anything untoward happens.'

'Hugh, do you know something you're not telling me?'

Hugh's smile was at its most charming. 'Client confidentiality and all that,' he said.

'But you know who the donor is?'

'He has expressed a desire to remain anonymous and it would be most unprofessional of me not to respect his wishes.'

'But he must be made to realise that if he changes his mind the decision could affect the lives of everyone at Ash Park. Can't you have a word with him — if you know who he is, that is,' Anna added, aware from the smug expression on Hugh's face that he was in full knowledge of the donor's identity.

'Do you know who he is, Hugh?' Anna said.

'Let's just say we like to keep these things in the family, if you get my drift.'

Anna gasped. What was Hugh saying? That Archie Wainright was the anonymous donor? But that would be a disaster!

Just then a loud burst of laughter from the far corner of the room caught everyone's attention. Anna saw her parents at the centre of the attention. They looked so happy. She couldn't stand by and see their happiness destroyed without doing something about it.

'I could perhaps have a word in his ear if you make it worth my while,' Hugh said.

'What are you saying exactly, Hugh?'

'I think you know.'

Hugh was standing very close to her now, so close that no-one could possibly overhear him. 'I'm in love with you Anna, and, unlike your friend, Phil Anderson, I'm prepared to go to any lengths for us to be together.'

'That's emotional blackmail.'

'Harsh words, Anna.'

'What would you call it, then? You want me to be nice to you in order for us not to lose the charity donation to Ash Park House?'

'I want more than that, Anna.' Hugh's vice was now so quiet Anna had to lean against him to fully hear what he was saying. 'I want you to marry me.'

Phil Knows About The Engagement

Phil was on the phone when Anna dashed into the office on Monday morning.

Her head throbbed and she knew her hair looked a sight. Neither had she had time to apply any make up. Both she and her father had slept through two alarm calls and then she'd had to run the last part of her journey to work from the bottom of the road where her father had dropped her off. He would have insisted on driving her all the way to the agency, but the rush hour traffic was so badly snarled up through the centre of town, she didn't want to make him even later than he already was.

'Sorry,' she mimed at Phil as she shrugged off her coat and began unlocking her desk. Hugh's ring knocked against the handles of the drawers. Anna shuddered and slipped it off her finger. It didn't belong there, but Hugh had insisted she wear his mother's engagement ring as a token of their relationship. Anna hadn't wanted anything as official as rings or announcements, but there had been no stopping Hugh.

Before the party had ended in the small hours of Sunday morning, he had made sure Celeste and George knew of his proposal and Anna's acceptance. Anna wasn't even sure she had accepted, but not wanting to make a scene, she had carried on smiling at the sea of faces as people swarmed round to congratulate her and Hugh. Inside she felt sick. But she couldn't bear the thought of what would happen to Ash Park House and her parents if she didn't go through with Hugh's plans.

Phil finished his telephone call and looked across at her.

'I understand congratulations are in order.' His voice was expressionless. 'When you rushed off on Saturday night, I didn't realise it was to get engaged to Hugh Wainwright.'

'Phil, I . . . ' she began, but he had turned away from her. 'We've a busy day in front of us. That was Jenny Barrow on the phone. She'll be coming in later to sign some papers.'

'The physio at Ash Park? That reminds me, she wanted to speak to you on Saturday night.'

Phil nodded. 'I've drawn up a contract and signed our copies. They only need Jenny's signature. Can you deal with it? I have to go out to Tindall's Farm. We've had an offer on the property.'

'That's wonderful news.'

'I doubt your future father-in-law would agree. Aren't you being just a bit disloyal to your new family?'

'I know what you must think of me,' Anna said quietly, 'but it isn't like that.'

'Well, I must say that you don't exactly look the blushing bride.' Phil softened his voice. 'Is something wrong?' His concern almost had her spilling out the truth. But she had sold herself to the highest bidder and the price was her parents' happiness. No way could she confess what she had done.

She shook her head. 'I'm probably tired, that's all. I didn't sleep very well last night.'

'Anna,' Phil frowned, 'if there's anything you want to tell me, I'm prepared to listen, if you'll trust me, and I promise, no strings attached.'

The tension in the air was palpable. The strain was almost proving too much for Anna. She couldn't look Phil in the eye. 'Really, there's nothing wrong,' she insisted.

'Has Hugh pressured you into this engagement?' Phil asked. 'It just all seemed so sudden.'

'He . . . we . . . ' Anna sought for the right words, but she couldn't find them without breaking her mother's trust.

'Anna, I know how loyal you can be, but you can tell me, you know. It wouldn't be breaking a trust.'

'I can't.' Anna shook her head.

'Your life hasn't been easy over the past few months, has it? And I don't think I made your situation any easier.'

Anna raised troubled eyes to meet his. 'No. That's not true,' she protested.

'You see, I expected you to be the spoilt daughter of a doting father, a father who forced me into giving you a job. I realised the deal wasn't going anywhere unless it included you, so,' Phil smiled ruefully, 'I reluctantly agreed to your father's terms. Then, when I first saw you, well, to put it bluntly, I was amazed. You were hard-working, compassionate and you cared about people.'

Anna's face was burning as she listened to Phil.

'I tried hard to find fault with everything you did, When I falsely accused you of being in cahoots with the Wainwrights, I didn't know the full facts, then when Valerie accidentally deleted those files and I suspected you, you didn't retaliate, but did something about retrieving them. It was then my conscience got the better of me and I realised what a fool I had been to pre-judge you and that I would never find another girl like you. I know there can never be anything between us, but I wanted you to know how I feel.'

'Phil,' Anna took a deep breath, 'don't say any more. Please.' She stood up. 'I have some photocopying to do.' She began to search through the files on her desk, anxious to find anything to copy, anything to get her away from Phil.

'Listen to me Anna,' Phil urged, 'your future happiness means so much to me.' He took a deep breath. 'You must not sacrifice it for your mother's sake.'

'My mother?' Anna stopped looking through her paperwork, her attention now focused on Phil.

'I know Celeste Eden is your mother. I've known for a while. I wouldn't be telling you now, but I've been talking to Celeste. She's not happy about your engagement to Hugh. And she doesn't know why you've promised to marry him. Are you sacrificing your future happiness for the sake of a promise that's not necessary?'

'No. I'm marrying Hugh because I want to.' Anna did her best to make her voice sound convincing, but the next moment she was in Phil's arms. Quite how it happened she didn't know.

His embrace enfolded her and she wanted to stay where she was forever. Phil's lips on hers were so gentle she thought she had imagined their touch. Then he drew away.

'No.' He pushed her gently away. 'I didn't mean that to happen.'

'Phil, please, I wanted it to happen, too.'

'Even though you're engaged to Hugh Wainwright?'

'Yes. No.' Anna shook her head.

'While you're still making up your mind what's going on in your life, I have a business to run.' He snatched up his leather jacket. 'Jenny will be here soon. The papers are on my desk. I'll leave you to finalise things.'

Anna's face was stinging from the sharpness of his words. 'Where are you going?'

'Hillcrest Farm. I may be tied up with the deal all day tomorrow as well, so don't expect me in the office.' And without another word, Phil strode out of the office.

★ ★ ★

Anna clung to the edge of her desk. She didn't think she was capable of standing up unaided. Her feelings were in turmoil. Phil knew that Celeste Eden was her mother. But that wasn't her problem any more. Archie Wainwright was. Did Phil know Archie was the benefactor of Ash Park House? It was the type of information that wouldn't remain confidential for long in a close community like Ashton Vale.

Hugh couldn't always be relied upon to be discreet. He might have found the temptation to tell other people too much. If Phil knew, maybe he would understand her position and why she had acted as she had.

Lost in a turmoil of thoughts, Anna didn't hear the bell on the door as someone pushed it open.

'Sorry. Didn't mean to interrupt.' Jenny hovered in the doorway. 'Is it all right if I come in?'

Anna removed her hand from the desk and tried to look business-like. 'Jenny. Hello. Come in.'

'I'm afraid I've only just arrived myself.'

'If it's inconvenient, I could come back later?'

'No, that's OK. Let's have some coffee and you call tell me what's been happening with the ransom strip.'

'It's all been under wraps. I wasn't sure the deal would go through until the last moment. I'm sorry I couldn't tell you before, Anna, only it was a delicate situation.'

Anna settled Jenny down in one of the visitors' chairs, then made the coffee.

'Do you know my father is Samuel

Tindall's brother?' Jenny said.

'Valerie mentioned something about it to me.'

'It was my father, Jack, who owned the ransom strip. I didn't know it myself until recently. Well, to cut a long story short, Phil offered to buy the piece of land off me. We didn't want Archie Wainwright getting his hands on it.' Jenny hesitated. 'I'm sorry. Now you're almost part of the Wainwright family, I shouldn't be speaking to you like this.'

'Nonsense. I'm as delighted as you are. Phil's gone up to Hillcrest Farm now. He's had an offer on the property.'

'So much seems to be happening at the moment, I can't get my head round it all. Celeste being taken on by an agent. Ash Park being saved. The farm sold. And then there's your engagement to Hugh . . . ' Her words trailed away. 'Anna, are you OK? You're looking very pale.'

'Lack of sleep, I think. Sorry. I'll just get your file.'

'Anna,' Jenny confessed, 'I saw you with Phil just now. You looked very . . . close.'

'There's nothing between Phil and myself,' Anna said quickly.

'I wasn't the only one who saw the two of you together. These windows are large and they give out onto the street. You were in his arms, Anna. You were seen. People will talk.'

'It's none of their business.'

'They'll make it their business when they see Anna Villiers in an embrace with Phil Armstrong the day after she has announced her engagement to Hugh Wainwright.'

Anna sagged against the back of her seat as the implication of Jenny's words sank in.

'You don't love Hugh, do you?' Jenny held up a hand. 'Don't answer that. I can see it in your eyes that you don't. But why on earth did you get engaged to him if you don't love him?'

'I had to,' Anna said bleakly. 'His father's the one who put up the money for the Ash Park House project and if I don't agree to the engagement, he's going to pull out.'

'What?' Jenny exploded.

'Hugh told me on Saturday night.'

'That his father was the benefactor of Ash Park House?'

Anna nodded. 'So you see, what else could I do? And the next thing I knew, he was telling everyone we were engaged and people were congratulating me. He's even given me a ring, an heirloom that's been in his family for generations.'

Jenny looked at Anna across the desk. 'Answer me this question honestly. Do you love Phil?'

'I,' Anna hesitated. There was no point in denying it any longer. 'Yes,' she admitted.

'Then tell him.'

'How can I? I'm engaged to Hugh.'

'It's not a proper engagement.'

'It's binding and there are conditions.'

'You make it sound like a contract.

What conditions?'

'The future of Ash Park House, for a start. I told you.'

'Anna, you have to speak to Phil about this. It's important. I can't say any more, but please, don't go through with your engagement to Hugh for the sake of Ash Park House.'

'I would never forgive myself if the Ash Park deal fell through because of me. Lives would be ruined.'

'It won't and they wouldn't. Hugh has no hold over you.' Jenny looked at the ornate ring Anna had placed on her desk. 'Give it back, Anna. I promise you it's the right thing to do. Then you must speak to Phil. Tell him what you've told me.'

'I can't.'

Jenny stood up. 'You must.'

'Where are you going?' Anna asked.

'I'm due on duty.'

'But you haven't signed your paper-work.'

Jenny flashed her a smile. 'And I don't intend to until you've spoken to Phil.'

Anna Has Words
With Hugh

'I suppose I was living in a dream world,' Hugh admitted as he looked at the ring nestling in the palm of his hand.

He and Anna were walking through Ash Meadow. 'I'm sorry, Hugh. I can't go through with the engagement, no matter what the consequences will be and I really don't think you've got it in you to jeopardise the future of Ash Park because of me.'

'You won't will you?' she begged. 'You know we wouldn't have been happy together.'

'It's Phil, isn't it?' Hugh's voice was resigned.

'Yes,' Anna admitted. If nothing else, Hugh deserved the truth, a truth that she had only just come to terms with herself. 'At least, on my part. He — well, he doesn't feel the same way about me.'

'Then he's a fool.' Hugh's voice was sharp.

'No,' Anna said softly, 'he isn't. It's me. I should have been more honest with him. But,' she shrugged, 'well it doesn't matter now.'

★   ★   ★

Jenny had been adamant that Anna's broken engagement to Hugh would not endanger Ash Park. But now Anna had taken the plunge, she wasn't so sure. Had she put the future of Ash Wood and Ash Meadow at risk? Not to mention the residents of Ash Park House and the planned therapy centre.

'Even if I'd never met Phil Anderson, there could never have been anything between us apart from childhood friendship, could there?' Anna said, in an attempt to soften the blow for Hugh.

'On your part maybe,' Hugh said.

'I'm not the girl for you,' Anna insisted. 'We live in different worlds these days.'

'I could become part of your world if you'd let me,' Hugh said eagerly, the light of hope rekindled in his eyes.

Anna shook her head. 'I don't think so. We have different — values.'

Hugh looked contrite. 'I admit I behaved foolishly, irresponsibly, forcing you into an engagement you didn't want. It was a stupid thing to do. You don't think too badly of me, Anna, do you?'

'No, I don't,' she replied softly.

'I wouldn't have seen through my threat about pulling the plug on Ash Park House. It was a moment's madness. I suppose I got carried away by all the excitement of the day. I'm sorry if I caused you any distress.'

'Hugh, there's no need to go on, I understand.'

'No. You don't. I'm not proud of the way I behaved and I owe it to you to put you right on certain things.'

'It's all right, Hugh. You've explained everything.'

'No, I haven't. You see, I couldn't have carried through my threat about removing the funding from Ash Park House because my father is not the anonymous donor.'

'He's not?' Anna stared at him. 'Then why did you say he was?'

'I didn't, not in so many words. I just let you think he was because it was the only way I thought I could get you to accept my proposal. I could see the way things were developing between you and Phil Anderson even if you couldn't, so I thought maybe I could get in before he staked his claim, as it were. I had to act quickly. So I seized my chance.'

'Hugh, there is nothing between Phil and myself. You know that.'

'You can't deny the pair of you were cosying up together at the auction all afternoon and the moment it was over you sneaked away together. I saw you. So it wasn't unnatural to jump to the conclusion that there was something going on.'

'But Phil would have stayed on for the party if there had been.'

'I guessed you might have had words with him and that was the real reason why he wasn't there. I should have known I was living on false hopes. Can you ever forgive me?'

'There is nothing to forgive.'

Anna looked at the disconsolate Hugh and felt a stirring of sorrow for him. She did love him, but as a brother.

'It was foolish of me to think you would have carried out your threat to evict all the residents of Ash Park,' Anna admitted. 'I should have known better.'

'Your mother was very good to me before her accident. I never knew my own mother, so she sort of took her place. Then, after what happened, I felt I owed it to her to help look after you.' He smiled slowly. 'I know I was only five years older than you, but I was your surrogate big brother.'

'And you did a wonderful job,' Anna smiled, then added, 'but Hugh, I'm no longer the little girl who ran round after you begging to be allowed to play football with you.'

'I realise that now.'

It felt natural to link her fingers with Hugh's as they strolled along.

'So if your father isn't the one putting up the funding for Ash Park, then who is?' Anna asked.

'I've no idea,' Hugh admitted. 'My father's lost all interest in the project now and he's moved on to other things.'

They walked on in silence for a few minutes.

'You know,' Hugh looked round, 'I'm pleased the development isn't going through. And it's not easy being the son of the town's most mistrusted citizen, you know.

'He is my father and I love him, but I think the time has come for me to move on. If I don't, I'll always be in his shadow, and I don't want that.'

'I think you're making the right decision.'

'Have you any idea of what you'll do?'

'I've got one or two friends with ideas of setting up our own company. Then there's the private allowance from my mother's family. It's not a fortune, but it's enough to see me through for the time being. It's still early days, of course, so we'll see. What about you? What are your plans?'

'I don't know. When my contract with Anderson Villiers comes to an end, I shall have to start job hunting.' Anna smiled at Hugh. 'And no thank you, I don't want a position working for you or your father.'

'I thought you'd say that,' Hugh grinned. 'Anyway,' he went on, 'my father's thinking of moving out of the area now the Ashton deal has fallen through.'

'Where will he go?'

'He may go abroad. There's a new project he's set his sights on in South

Africa. He was talking to Jenny Barrow's father about it at the Open Day.'

'Ashton Vale will miss him.'

Hugh cast her a sideways look. 'You mean like an aching tooth?'

'I suppose I do.' Now she no longer had the shadow of her engagement hanging over her, Anna felt free to laugh. She breathed in the scent of the early evening air, enjoying the memories of childhood it invoked.

'So,' Hugh said, 'it looks like this really is the parting of the ways.'

'Hugh?' Anna said with a twinge of sadness.

'Yes?'

'I don't think I've ever said it before, but thank you. For everything.'

No more words were necessary.

Anna knew they were both thinking about the night her mother had fallen off her horse and how the young Hugh had comforted Anna, never leaving her side.

Then, during the dark days that

followed he had been there for her, offering her a ride on his new bike and buying her sweets out of his pocket money. He had let her cry in his arms and then wiped the tears off her cheeks with a muddy handkerchief.

A year or so later he'd taken the blame when Anna had fallen off the garden wall and cut her head so badly she still bore the scar. They'd both known it had been Anna showing off that had caused the accident, but ever since her mother's accident her grandfather had taken to berating her for the slightest thing, and Hugh knew she would be in trouble if Robert Villiers had found out what had really happened. So he took the blame.

'You'll always have the scar to remember me by.' Hugh stroked her hairline.

For a moment Anna thought he might try to kiss her. Before he could, she stepped away from him and her movement broke the spell between them.

'Right,' Hugh said with a brisk smile, 'can I leave you to walk back home alone?'

Anna raised her eyebrows at the abruptness of his tone.

'What happened to the friends for life thing?' she teased, a little bit put out.

'You'll have Dixie for company, and I've got a date tonight.'

'Already? I thought you were nursing a broken heart.'

'It'll mend.' Hugh's smile was a shadow of its old self but there were to be no emotional scenes, for which Anna was grateful. 'It's college reunion night and those friends I mentioned have promised to be there, so I should sound them out and see what's happening.'

'Good idea.'

'Besides, I half promised Valerie I'd take her along,' Hugh admitted.

'You're taking Valerie Masters to the college reunion?'

'Yes.'

'Even though when you asked her you were engaged to me?' Anna's voice rose in disbelief.

'To be honest, I suspected the reason you suggested going for a walk this evening was because you'd found me out for the liar I was. I was expecting my marching orders.'

'So you lined up a reserve? Nice one, Hugh.'

'Don't think any the worse of me, Anna. If you had accepted my proposal properly you would have made me the happiest man on this earth, but my intuition told me it wasn't to be. I mean, if you had really loved me, it wouldn't have been necessary for me to blackmail you into accepting my engagement ring, would it?'

'Sometimes you are very like your father, Hugh. He's got all the answers, too.'

'You can come to the do if you like,' Hugh suggested.

'No, I don't think Valerie would thank me for that. Now you'd better get going if you don't want to be late.'

'I suppose I should be on my way.'

'And do my eyes deceive me, or is that Valerie walking towards us now?' Anna shaded her eyes against the dying sunlight to where an elegant figure was picking her way daintily over the meadow.

'Why, yes.' Hugh looked genuinely surprised, 'So it is.'

Anna noticed how his face lit up at the sight of Valerie and felt a small glow of warmth. Perhaps things would work out for them.

'What on earth is she doing here?' Hugh said.

'Coming to check up on us, I expect,' Anna laughed. 'Go on,' she nudged Hugh. 'If Valerie is the girl for you we don't want any further misunderstandings.'

'She's out of a job now, too, so I've got to look after her, haven't I?' Hugh said.

Anna nodded. 'You'll be good at it, Hugh, and Valerie needs you.'

Hugh hesitated. 'We could all walk back together, if you like.'

'No, I need some time alone to sort out my thoughts.' Anna waved at Valerie who had come to a halt in front of a stile.

'Hugh, I don't think Valerie's shoes are up to going any further and she could be seriously undignified if she attempts the stile in that skirt, so off you go.' She kissed Hugh on the cheek. 'Keep in touch?'

'I will. Goodbye, Anna.'

Anna watched Hugh walk away towards his new girlfriend. Seeing them together, she realised they were right for each other.

'Dixie?' Anna whistled. 'Where are you?'

Her cry was greeted with a bout of happy barking and Dixie, ears lolling, came racing out of the undergrowth towards her.

'We are going to walk until our legs are too tired to move another step, Dixie. Are you up for it?'

Dixie barked back at her and ran off in the direction of Ash Wood. After a few moments Anna began to trudge after her.

Towards A Bright Future

Anna's father was hovering in the porch outside Mallards. He hurried towards her. 'Where have you been? It's almost dark. I was about to send out a search party.'

'I went for a long walk with Dixie.'

'Well you've got a visitor.'

'Who is it?'

It was then Anna noticed the four-wheel drive parked under the oak tree.

'Phil Anderson,' her father said unnecessarily. 'He's been here for hours. I'm running out of things to say to him and we've both drunk far more coffee than is good for us. I'm awash with the stuff.'

George hustled Anna into the vestibule.

She glanced in the mirror above the hallstand and almost bit down a shriek.

The damp evening air had done a good job of dissolving her mascara. Two black marks had trickled down her cheeks, and her hair was sporting what looked like half a tree. Bits of undergrowth had become entangled when she'd stopped Dixie from disappearing down a rabbit hole.

'You'll have to hold the fort a bit longer, Dad,' Anna said, ignoring the rapid beating of her heart. Whatever it was Phil Anderson had to say to her would have to wait until she had made herself presentable. There wasn't time for a shower but she needed to wash her face, comb her hair and change out of her mud-spattered jeans and T-shirt.

'Don't take forever,' George hissed at his daughter. 'In the meantime I'll make myself scarce. Come on, Dixie. What has your mistress been doing to you? You need a bit of attention, too.'

Dixie pattered happily after George and the pair of them headed towards the kitchen.

Anna raced up to her room. She wasn't in the least vain, but if this visit from Phil Anderson was going to be the challenging one she suspected it would be, then she at least wanted to look clean.

After quickly washing her face, she chose a crisp white newly-laundered T-shirt and black velvet trousers. She combed back her hair. Without make-up, her scar was more prominent than usual but Anna wasn't in the mood to worry about it. Hugh had never found her scar in the slightest bit unsightly and tonight Phil Anderson would see her as she was.

'OK, Dad. I'm ready.' She poked her head round the kitchen door to where her father was busy attending to Dixie's muddy paws.

'You look lovely, Annie,' he said, smiling at her.

★ ★ ★

Anna nudged open the study door. It was a cosy room and its shabby untidiness bore evidence of its use on a daily basis.

'Hello.' She breezed in. 'I'm sorry you had to wait so long. I went for a walk across Ash Meadow. With Hugh Wainwright,' she added, in a fit of defiance. She tilted her chin and waited for Phil's reaction.

Like Anna, he had dressed casually, in pale blue shirt and jeans. The expression on his face was unreadable. The silence between them grew uncomfortable.

'Er — were we expecting you?' Anna finally asked, when he didn't say anything.

'No,' was all he said.

'Then may I know why you're here?' Anna said, annoyed to find herself wrong-footed. She had rather hoped Phil would be more forthcoming. As it was, she was the one doing all the talking.

'I called because,' Phil paused,

263

'you're not wearing your engagement ring.'

Anna flexed the bare fingers of her left hand. 'Hugh and I have broken off our engagement.'

'I see.'

Anna wished it were autumn. They always lit a fire in the evening when the nights drew in and stoking the coals was a task she enjoyed. It gave her something to do with her hands and right now she desperately needed a distraction. 'Tindall's Farm?' she asked, as another silence fell between them.

'What about it?'

'Is that why you're here, to update me on the deal? I checked my voice mail but there were no messages.'

'No, Tindall's Farm isn't the reason I'm here.' He looked directly into her eyes. 'I'm here because I've had Jenny Barrow on the phone, begging me to speak to you to stop you marrying Hugh Wainright.'

'Jenny?' Anna feigned innocence, 'why would she do that?'

'She seemed to think I was in danger of sullying your reputation in the town.' Phil's lips twitched. 'I gather we put on a bit of a floorshow for the local residents yesterday — if it is possible to put on a floorshow in a shop window.'

Anna flushed, unable to look him in the eye.

'That's ridiculous,' she addressed the floor.

'Ridiculous or not, word has apparently got round that you and I were indulging in, shall we say, inappropriate behaviour.'

'If we ignore the rumours, they'll soon stop,' Anna said. 'And you haven't come here to tell me about a little local gossip, have you? I mean, rivetting though that nugget of information is, it could have waited until Monday morning.'

'I agree, but Jenny was also jabbering on about you getting engaged to Hugh because of his father and Ashton House. I couldn't really understand it all, but she sounded anxious and insisted I see you as soon as possible. Do you have any idea what she was talking about?'

'It's to do with the ransom strip, I think. She didn't complete the paperwork. She said she wasn't going to seal the deal until I'd spoken to you. Phil,' Anna went on, 'don't keep looking at me like that. I did my best . . . '

Phil was across the room in two strides. 'Blow Jenny's paperwork. That's not why I'm here.'

'It is. You said . . . '

'I know what I said.' Phil pulled her towards him. 'Even if Jenny hadn't spoken to me I would have come here to beg you to break off your engagement.'

'Why?' Anna held her breath as she waited for his answer.

'Because I want you to marry me, instead.'

Her racing heart left Anna feeling weak at the knees. 'Would you mind repeating that?'

'Will you marry me?' Phil said.

'Yes,' Anna said simply.

266

Phil kissed her and it was several moments before they drew apart.

★ ★ ★

'I love you, Anna,' Phil said softly. 'You've no idea of the torment I've been going through. When I told your father of my intentions tonight and asked him if it was all right for me to ask for your hand, he said he wasn't sure if you would accept me. I've been on tenterhooks for hours. I tell you, Anna, I was on the verge of searching the woods for you, and if I'd found you and Hugh Wainwright there together, I think I might have hit him.'

'Why are you laughing?' Phil demanded. 'I'm telling you I love you madly and all you can do is laugh.'

'I'm laughing because I'm so happy,' Anna said. 'I was dreading the day I would have to leave work, knowing I might never see you again.'

Phil kissed her again. 'You've no idea how often I've wanted to do that, but every time I tried to get close to you, you turned away from me.'

'I had to. There were so many complications,' Anna said, as she lent against his chest.

'They're all over now,' he said, his words tickling her hair.

Anna looked up into his eyes. 'But you have to tell me what's going on. Why is Jenny acting the way she is?'

'It's difficult to know where to start, but you should know that Archie Wainwright is not Ash Park's mysterious benefactor.'

'I realise that now, but on the night of Celeste's party, Hugh told me he was, at least he led me to believe he was. That's why we got engaged. He said that if I didn't agree to his proposal, he'd make sure the money wasn't forthcoming.'

'I'd like to wring his neck.' Phil began to look angry again, 'and if I ever set eyes on him in the future, I think I might.'

'Don't,' Anna implored him. 'Hugh

and I have had things out. He realised it was a stupid thing to do. He's sorry.'

'He could have ruined your life.'

'It wouldn't have come to that. I'd made up my mind to return his ring.'

'I suppose that father of his was behind it.'

'I don't know,' Anna said, 'and it doesn't matter any more; it's in the past. Let's talk about the future — our future.'

'And you're really sure you want to marry me?'

'I've never been more certain about anything in my life,' Anna said softly. 'And if you want to hear me say it again, then, I love you. Does that satisfy you?'

'I'll be the perfect husband, I promise.'

'Don't be. I'd go mad if you were perfect. I don't want a perfect anything. I want you, as you are.' Anna hesitated. 'But do you want me as I am?' she said, pushing up her hair to reveal her childhood scar.

Phil kissed her forehead. 'You're beautiful, Anna Villiers, and I want you just as you are. Forever.'

* * *

'If it wasn't Archie Wainwright who funded the Ash Park House project, then who was it?' Anna asked Phil.

'It was me,' Phil said quietly.

'You?' Anna repeated.

'With Jenny's input. She used some of the money she made from the sale of her land and between us we came up with an appropriate figure.'

'Why didn't you say anything?' Anna felt an irrational jealousy at the thought of Jenny and Phil working together on a scheme that had excluded her.

'The deal couldn't be finalised until the Tindalls accepted the offer on their property. That's what I've been working on all day.'

'You could have told me.'

'You had your secrets, too,' Phil reminded her.

'And does Celeste know about any of this?' Anna asked.

'No-one knows, apart from Jenny, Andy and the trustees. You're the first person I've told.' Phil pulled Anna to him again, and for the next few minutes all thoughts of Ash Park vanished as they sealed their love with the sweetest of kisses.

Eventually they drew apart and Anna said, 'Can we tell my father our news?'

But at that moment the door slowly opened and George came into the room.

'I'm sorry. I couldn't wait to find out what was happening. But I take it from your expressions that she said yes, then, Phil?' Anna and Phil both nodded happily at him.

'Congratulations, my darling.' George hugged her and Dixie barked round her ankles. 'And Phil, welcome to the family.'

'And,' he added, 'if you should be looking for somewhere to honeymoon, Celeste and I would recommend the Villa St Helena.'

'The Italian Lake,' Anna said softly, 'that's where it all began, wasn't it?'

'And I can't think of a better place to finish, can you?' Phil said.

'No, I really can't,' Anna replied, and lifted her face for a kiss from the man she knew she truly loved with all her heart.

THE END

We do hope that you have enjoyed reading this large print book.

Did you know that all of our titles are available for purchase?

We publish a wide range of high quality large print books including:
Romances, Mysteries, Classics
General Fiction
Non Fiction and Westerns

Special interest titles available in large print are:
The Little Oxford Dictionary
Music Book, Song Book
Hymn Book, Service Book

Also available from us courtesy of Oxford University Press:
Young Readers' Dictionary
(large print edition)
Young Readers' Thesaurus
(large print edition)

For further information or a free brochure, please contact us at:
Ulverscroft Large Print Books Ltd.,
The Green, Bradgate Road, Anstey,
Leicester, LE7 7FU, England.
Tel: (00 44) **0116 236 4325**
Fax: (00 44) **0116 234 0205**

Other titles in the
Linford Romance Library:

THE ECHOING BELLS

Lillie Holland

In Germany Marnie Burness accepts the post of governess at Schloss Beissel. Her charge is Count von Oldenburg's daughter, Charlotte. Despite finding much to disapprove of at the Schloss, against her own principles she falls in love with the Count. Then, when Maria, the Count's wife, is murdered Marnie suspects his involvement. She leaves the Schloss, but will she ever learn the truth about the death of the countess — and will her suspicions of the Count be proved right?